Praise for
Valerie Wolzien
and her novels

"A nice writing style and considerable wit."
—*Chicago Tribune*

"Wit is Wolzien's strong suit. . . . Her portrayal of small-town life will prompt those of us in similar situations to agree that we too have been there and done that."
—*The Mystery Review*

"Domestic mysteries, with their emphasis on everyday people and everyday events, are very popular and the Susan Henshaw stories are some of the best in this subgenre."
—*Romantic Times*

By Valerie Wolzien
(published by The Random House Publishing Group)

Susan Henshaw mysteries:
MURDER AT THE PTA LUNCHEON
THE FORTIETH BIRTHDAY BODY
WE WISH YOU A MERRY MURDER
AN OLD FAITHFUL MURDER
ALL HALLOW'S EVIL
A STAR-SPANGLED MURDER
A GOOD YEAR FOR A CORPSE
'TIS THE SEASON TO BE MURDERED
REMODELED TO DEATH
ELECTED FOR DEATH
WEDDINGS ARE MURDER
THE STUDENT BODY
DEATH AT A DISCOUNT
AN ANNIVERSARY TO DIE FOR
DEATH IN A BEACH CHAIR
DEATH IN DUPLICATE

Josie Pigeon mysteries:
SHORE TO DIE
PERMIT FOR MURDER
DECK THE HALLS WITH MURDER
THIS OLD MURDER
MURDER IN THE FORECAST
A FASHIONABLE MURDER
DEATH AT A PREMIUM

DEATH AT A PREMIUM

 A JOSIE PIGEON MYSTERY

VALERIE WOLZIEN

FAWCETT

BALLANTINE BOOKS · NEW YORK

A Fawcett Books Mass Market Original

Copyright © 2005 by Valerie Wolzien

Published in the United States by Fawcett Books, an imprint of The Random House Publishing Group, a division of Random House, Inc., New York.

FAWCETT BOOKS and colophon are trademarks of Random House, Inc.

ISBN 0-345-46809-0

Cover illustration: Dave Calver

Printed in the United States of America

www.ballantinebooks.com

OPM   9 8 7 6 5 4 3 2 1

This book is dedicated to Katherine Hall Page—
fine writer and good friend.

ONE

THERE ARE WOMEN for whom being engaged is a wonderful time. The long search for the perfect wedding gown, veil, and shoes is a joy. Hours spent with floral designers, photographers, and musicians are happy and productive. These women delight in finding the best venue for the service and their reception. They review menus with caterers time and time again, hoping to devise the perfect meal for their guests. They even find the wording on the invitation of compelling interest.

Josie Pigeon didn't get it. "I still don't understand why we can't just elope," she said to Sam Richardson, her fiancé.

Sam was a reasonable man. "We can. We can do anything you want to do."

"You said Carol is already shopping for the perfect dress."

"You know perfectly well that my mother doesn't need an excuse to shop."

"I think Tyler might be looking forward to escorting me down the aisle."

"Your son will do whatever you want him to do, and then he'll get right back to the serious task of selecting a college. Seniors in high school are not all that interested in weddings."

"My parents would probably prefer a traditional service."

"How many years has it been since you let their priorities rule your life?"

Josie twisted her long red hair into a knot at the back of her neck, then let it drop over her shoulders again. "We don't have to make these decisions now."

"You've been saying that for the past four months—Island Contracting's slow period," Sam reminded her. "Now that your busy season is about to begin, it's going to be more difficult to find the time to do all this."

They were sitting in Josie's office—a remodeled fishing shack that jutted out over the bay on the barrier island both of them called home. It was early morning and Josie was finishing off one of the glazed doughnuts she loved. Sam was munching just as happily on a rice cake. He looked relaxed. Josie was nervous. Today she would learn whether she would get the big job which would carry her business through the summer season.

Island Contracting was a year-round business, but in the winter the crew dwindled down to one or two people and the jobs were mostly local fixups or quick storm damage repairs. Summer was her big season, and if she got the job she was hoping for, this could be her last leisurely morning until Labor Day weekend.

Josie glanced over Sam's shoulder at the wall calendar. September was hidden beneath May, June, July, and August, but she knew Labor Day was circled in red. It was going to be their wedding day. Sam was right: she had to make some decisions soon.

Her resolve lasted all of six seconds, until the phone on her desk rang. She grabbed for the receiver.

"Island Contracting. Josie Pigeon speaking."

Sam got up and wandered out onto the small deck suspended over the bay. Wire crab traps were piled high, waiting for the blue crabs to appear as the water warmed, and leaving only enough space for two rickety old captain's chairs. He sat down and stared out at the water. He could hear Josie's conversation through the open doorway, and her tone told him what he wanted to know before her appearance confirmed it.

"I got the job! Island Contracting is going to remodel the Bride's Secret Bed and Breakfast." She flopped down in the other chair.

"Congratulations. When do you start?"

"As soon as possible. I'll go look the place over today. The blueprints are waiting at the municipal center. The permits have been issued. All I have to do is hire a crew and order supplies, and we can get to work. The new owner wants the work completed this summer."

"When is Nic coming back?" Sam asked.

"Sometime this afternoon. She planned to leave the convention early this morning and the drive up from D.C.—shouldn't take more than three or four hours, right?"

Sam nodded. "Depending on traffic, of course."

"I promised I'd talk to her before I hired any workers."

"Why?"

"The whole point of the convention is to get women in the construction industry together. She expected to see a lot of old friends there, and she was hoping to talk some of them into moving here for the summer to work for Island Contracting."

"You're letting someone else hire your crew? That doesn't sound like you."

"It isn't. And I'm not, but I did say I would give her friends a chance. Nic's a great finish carpenter. We've done some good work this winter. I don't think she would bring women to see me unless they were first-rate."

"I know how much you like Nic, Josie . . ."

"And you don't." Josie knew she sounded impatient, but they had had this discussion many times in the past few months, and each time she ended up feeling like a teenager whose parents were criticizing her friends. This feeling was one of the unfortunate side effects of being in love with a man almost twenty years her senior. In truth, she knew Sam had her best interests at heart, but damn it, Nic was a good worker and responsible as well. Josie knew that Sam thought Nic was too self-centered and not concerned enough about her or Island Contracting, but she had never seen any evidence of that, and besides, good finish carpenters were hard to find. She opened her mouth to remind him of that fact when he made another suggestion.

"I have some free time this morning, and I'd love to see the inside of that old inn."

Josie laughed. "I gather you've never been there."

"No. Why? It's a classic shingle-style shore cottage. I've always thought it so charming when I drive by . . ."

"The charm is barely skin deep. It was converted into a bed and breakfast in the mid-sixties by someone with no taste, and no one's spent a dime on it since then. The interior is appalling. But I'd love to have company," she added, smiling over at him.

"Do you have to pick up a key?"

"No, I went over the place before I put in my bid. The key is still in my desk."

"I'll help you look. You probably want to find it before Labor Day."

Josie glanced over at him. She knew he was kidding, but she didn't need to be reminded of her lack of organizational skills. "Actually, it's in the top left-hand drawer—under my computer." She didn't need to admit that the only reason she could speak so confidently was that she had spent at least an hour searching for it the afternoon before.

Sam stood up. "Let's take my car. I have the top down."

Josie grinned. "If it's fresh air you want, you could ride in the back of my truck."

"I think I'll stick to my hand-tanned glove leather."

"Wimp."

"Just as long as I'm the wimp you love," he said.

The key was where Josie expected to find it, and in a few minutes they were on their way to the north end of the island. As Sam had promised, the top of his classic MGB was down. Josie turned on the radio and found an oldies station playing "Hey Jude." Only when the song had ended did they hear the siren of the police car behind them. Sam cursed quietly and pulled over to the side of the wide empty boulevard. He turned off his engine and looked at Josie.

"Asshole."

Sam knew she wasn't referring to him. They heard footsteps and turned in their seats, expecting either Mike Rodney or his father—the police presence on the island during the off season—so the tall blonde goddess strutting toward the MGB came as a complete surprise.

"Nice car." She placed one hand on the door and leaned down to get a closer look at the dashboard. "Nineteen sixty-seven?"

"Sixty-six," Sam answered.

Josie noticed he was smiling. "Is anything the matter, Officer?" she asked a bit too loudly.

The woman answered her question looking at Sam. "The island speed limit is twenty-five miles per hour. You were traveling at almost forty."

"You must be new to the island. Generally, in the off-season, the traffic rules are relaxed a bit."

"I may be *new* here, but as an attorney, surely you're aware of the fact that laws are not generally open to seasonal variations," she added, putting emphasis on the repeated word.

Josie spoke up. "How do you know Sam's a lawyer?"

"Someone mentioned it to me," the police officer answered without taking her eyes off Sam.

"Who?" Josie demanded loudly.

The officer's cell phone rang. "Excuse me." She flipped the phone open and looked at the face. "Officer Trish Petric here."

There was a long pause while the caller made his wishes known, then with a quick, "Yes, sir!" the woman flipped her phone shut and returned her attention to Josie and Sam—or, it seemed to Josie, just Sam.

"I'll let you go with a warning, Mr. Richardson, but you might want to remember that Memorial Day is less than a week away."

"I'll do that, Officer Petric," Sam answered.

Josie noticed that he hadn't stopped smiling since

stopping the car. "That bitch!" she said when they were alone again. If she had expected her fiancé to agree— and she did—she was disappointed.

"She was right, you know," Sam said. "Those of us who live here year-round do tend to forget that the laws weren't designed for seasonal enforcement."

"But they were, Sam. The only reason for anyone to go twenty-five miles an hour on a road this wide is because it's full of people biking, jogging, and going to the beach. And that only happens in the summer. Right now there's no reason in the world that we shouldn't be going forty-five or even sixty miles an hour!"

Sam didn't argue, but whether that was because there were no other cars in sight or because they had arrived at their destination, Josie didn't know. He parked on the street in front of the Bride's Secret Bed and Breakfast and looked up at the building. There was a lot to look at.

The large symmetrical building faced the street with matching two-story towers on either end. A deep porch spanned the front of the house with steps at one end leading to wide French doors. Above the door, a second-floor sleeping porch filled the space between the towers. Dozens of many-paned windows embellished the first two floors. Three hipped gables jutted out of the mansard roof, each equipped with three identical shuttered windows. The shingles had weathered to a silvery gray in the island's salt-laden air. All trim had been painted glossy white.

"Fresh paint job?" Sam asked.

"Yes. The last owner's attempt to increase what Realtors call 'curb appeal' these days. And the curb is pretty much where the appeal stops."

The couple got out of the car and walked up the sidewalk toward the porch steps. The wooden porch floor hadn't been painted in years. An old, beat-up rattan welcome mat inadequately covered the threshold, and Josie tripped over a turned-up corner on her way to the door. She put the key in the lock and turned. The door wouldn't budge. She tried again with the same result. Sam took the key from her and tried. The door swung open.

"How did you do that?"

"It wasn't locked. When you turned it, you were actually making it impossible to get inside," Sam explained, waving her in the door before him.

"I wonder why it was left open."

Sam didn't respond to her statement. He was staring at the foyer walls, his mouth open, amazed by what he saw.

TWO

"**H**IDEOUS, ISN'T IT?"

"Actually, it's quite evocative," Sam answered, never taking his eyes off the huge pink and orange paisley design covering the walls.

Josie frowned. *Evocative* quite possibly would be the last word she would have used to describe this. Actually, when she thought about it, she couldn't remember ever describing anything as evocative.

"Reminds me of my college days," Sam continued. "I used to date a girl who had this wallpaper in her bedroom."

Josie knew Sam was going to enjoy his walk down memory lane and through the bedrooms of his youth a whole lot more than she would. "The living room is over there—through that arch."

Sam went where she indicated, and Josie, heading in the opposite direction toward the dining room and kitchen, could hear his amazed exclamation. She had had an identical reaction when confronted with the op art on the walls, the out-of-date furniture, and stained flokati rug on the floor, although she hadn't sounded nearly as appreciative.

The dining room was dominated by a glass and chrome

elliptical table surrounded by twelve white Plexiglas chairs. Josie thought it was horrible; she couldn't imagine why anyone would want to look at their own legs—or the legs of their tablemates—while eating, especially since the sight would be reflected endlessly in the mirror tiles lining the walls. Heavy linen curtains printed with thick waves of black, brown, and white hung in the bay window. The effect made her slightly seasick, so she continued into the kitchen—a nightmare of avocado appliances, fake walnut cabinetry, faux Mexican tile floors, worn orange Formica counter tops, and peeling metallic wallpaper.

Tripping over a cracked edge of linoleum, Josie pulled open the refrigerator. Cold air escaped and she closed it quickly. Good. A functioning kitchen would make the beginning of the remodel easier. There was even a tiny half bathroom around the corner. Avoiding another loose tile, she peeked in: pink and white paisley wall paper, pink and white octagonal tiles on the floor, a pink and purple striped shower curtain. Josie left the room and pulled the door closed before nausea struck.

Sam had followed her into the kitchen and was examining a row of enameled copper canisters on the counter top. "I remember when these things were popular—everyone I knew had a set."

Josie resisted the rising urge to make a sarcastic comment concerning the good old days.

"Is this whole place furnished?" he asked.

"Sure is. There's mainly old wicker stuff in the bedrooms, as well as what used to be known as campaign chests—remember those dressers with extra brass hardware on the corners? My mother stored out-of-season clothing in one up in our attic."

"Very swinging sixties," Sam said, nodding.

"And you won't believe the lamps. They hang over all the beds and some of the chests. They're all different but they're the strangest shapes."

"I can't wait to see them. Are they anything like the one over the dining room table?"

"No. They're made from colored glass—brightly colored glass. Come on, I'll show you."

Sam followed Josie up the stairs and they examined the bedrooms on the second floor, and then continued on to the third. "Actually, my favorite room is up here," she explained as they stood on the upper landing. She opened the first door they came to. "You'll need to duck your head. The ceiling's awfully low."

They were underneath the eaves and above the second-floor bay window. A window seat had been built beneath the three wide multipaned windows. Skylights pierced the roof and the room shimmered with light.

"No sixties furniture in here," Sam commented, bending down to look out the window. "Hey, you can see over the dunes to the ocean."

Josie nodded. "Nice, isn't it?"

"Very."

"There's a matching room at the back of the house, but some idiot turned it into a bathroom decades ago. There's a window seat there, but it's been covered with stained old Contact paper. I can't wait to remove it."

"This place is remarkably symmetrical: matching tower rooms on the second floor, the two eave rooms up here . . ."

"And the tops of the towers were turned into identical closets, one at either end of the hall here."

"This is going to be a huge private home," Sam commented, walking down the hallway and opening door after door.

"Yeah. It's been on the market for years. The couple who ran it as a bed-and-breakfast claimed to barely be paying the taxes and keeping the building standing on what they made taking in guests. But it seemed too big to sell for a private home. Everyone assumed whoever bought it would keep it as a bed-and-breakfast."

"Who did buy it?"

"Seymour and Tilly Higgins. I haven't met them, but apparently they're wealthy enough to buy this place and remodel it—and old enough to have six grandchildren to occupy all the bedrooms when they have family get-togethers. I just hope they have plenty of money and care about their family enough to do everything the right way."

"Well, the money's there. Seymour Higgins is one of the most influential men on Wall Street," Sam said.

"Rich?"

"Really, really rich."

"Good, because this place is going to need a lot of money to pull it out of the swinging sixties and into this century."

"Interesting that he's buying a place here rather than out in the Hamptons with the rest of the rich and famous."

"The island has sentimental value for them. He and his wife met here—apparently they both worked on the island one summer when they were in college."

"Where?"

"I don't know, but I'm meeting with Mrs. Higgins in a few weeks to review some of the finishing details. Maybe she'll tell me all about it then."

"That should be interesting," Sam said. He had lifted an orange vase off a hall table and was examining its base. "You know, these things are collectable."

"By who?" As soon as the words were out of her mouth, she began to wonder if *whom* was proper. Sam would know, of course, but he was too nice to correct her.

"There are lots of collectors of mid-century furniture and accessories," Sam answered without comment.

Josie didn't say anything. She didn't share Sam's fondness for anything made in the 1950s and '60s. Perhaps because she hadn't been born until almost two decades later. "Well, if Seymour Higgins is a big shot in financial circles, maybe he'll know where to sell them."

Sam was looking out a window.

"Can you see the bay from here?" Josie asked, joining him.

"No, but I was looking at the backyard. There's a three-stall garage out there."

"Yes, but there's only space for two cars. One of the stalls was converted to a laundry room. There are two washer and dryer combos as well as a bathroom. There's also an outdoor shower around back." She frowned.

"What's wrong?"

"I was wondering how the electric comes into the buildings. Maybe I can keep the power on there when the house is disconnected from the grid. I think I'll go down and check it out. Can you hang around a bit longer?"

"Sure, let's go take a look."

They went back downstairs, this time passing through the kitchen into the small pebble-strewn backyard. An old-fashioned wooden clothesline had once stood there.

Now its ropes, torn by winter storms, lay on the ground, clothespins still attached.

A door had been installed in the middle of one of the old-fashioned garage doors. Sam grabbed the knob and it opened easily. "This is unlocked too," he said.

Josie nodded. "But it may not have been unlocked for long. I know the architect's been here a few times—perhaps he left it open. We'll lock up before we leave."

Sam was no longer paying attention. The far wall of the garage was covered with car posters. "That's a Jaguar X-type. Probably nineteen sixty-four . . ." he said, moving toward them.

Josie, knowing how much Sam loved classic cars, left him to peruse the collection and continued into the laundry area. The layout was pretty much as she remembered it: the far wall was lined with a pair of washer and dryers. A pile of broken-down plastic laundry baskets had been dumped beneath the large, battered oak table which dominated the middle of the room. Josie was examining the bank of outlets on the wall behind the appliances when Sam joined her.

"That's one of the best collections of sixties car posters I've ever run into. Too bad no one took care of them: in good shape, they'd be worth some real money."

"Why don't you take them? I'm thinking of setting up a table saw out here. A thick layer of sawdust won't increase their value."

Sam frowned. "I can't just remove things without the owner's permission."

"It's just a few old posters."

"They do belong to someone though, and they need to be protected. Maybe you could take them down and put them somewhere safe before you begin work."

"Maybe." Josie wasn't going to promise anything. "Look, we're going to have to empty the house before we start demolition. We could put a bunch of the furniture in this bay and cover it with heavy tarps . . ."

"That's a good idea. I'm no expert in mid-century furniture, but I believe some of those lamps you hate so much are Holmegaard glass—popular in the sixties and not cheap even then. If they are Holmgaard, they're worth real money to collectors."

Josie frowned. "Not good news," she announced.

"Why not?"

"Because when they were worthless, I was going to toss them in a pile, cover them up and forget about them. Now they'll have to be protected until someone in the Higgins family figures out what to do with them. Clearing the place will take an extra day or two—I hate to get behind schedule early on a job."

"You don't even have a crew for this one."

"That's not going to be a problem!" she protested and glanced down at her watch. "In fact, Nic should be arriving back soon. As soon as I talk to her, I'll know who I need to look for. I'll call around, and Island Contracting should be up and running in a day or two. You know I rarely have trouble finding workers."

"There's an awful lot of building going on on the island this summer and more than one new construction company," Sam pointed out. "Basil said he couldn't find a free plumber when a pipe broke in one of his kitchens over the weekend."

"Really?" Josie sounded doubtful for the first time. "I wonder who he called . . . Did you hear something outside?" she asked, interrupting herself.

"Just shouting. Probably neighborhood kids."

"I don't know why neighborhood kids would be calling my name," Josie said, starting toward the doorway and using her hand to shield her eyes from the bright sun. "I think . . . Oh, god, it must be Nic. She drives the only purple pick-up on the island. She's probably in the house looking for me. I'll be right back," she promised.

Fifteen minutes passed before she returned to the garage. Sam, who had kept himself amused browsing through a pile of old car magazines he had discovered in a corner beside a rusting hot water heater, was surprised by the expression on his fiancé's face: she was scowling.

"What's wrong?"

"I think I have a problem . . . a legal problem."

"Finally something I can help you with." He stood up. "What exactly is wrong?"

"I . . . Well, you're not going to like this, but you know I told Nic to go ahead and offer jobs to a few people on my approval. I trust her, and she was going to be seeing old friends—women she had worked with before. Well, it never occurred to me that there might be a problem. After all, the convention she was attending was for women in the construction industry . . . it never occurred to me . . ." She stopped speaking.

"What never occurred to you? Did she offer someone a job—someone you don't want to hire?"

"Exactly. Could that be a problem?"

"Probably not. I assume whoever was looking for a job understood that you have the final say . . ."

Josie nodded vigorously. "Of course."

"So, if you think one of the people Nic wants isn't qualified to work for Island Contracting, I can't imagine that there would be a legal problem. You have the final say over who you hire."

"We already agreed to that," Josie pointed out.

"Unless of course you don't want to hire them because you don't like their race or religion."

"And that would be illegal, wouldn't it?"

"It would be, but it doesn't sound like you, Josie. You've never seemed at all prejudiced and you've hired lots of minorities. What's the problem?"

"A man. Nic inadvertently offered a job at Island Contracting to a man. An exceptionally good-looking man. And he flirts."

"Then, my dear, you just might have a few problems—not all of them legal."

THREE

TWO DAYS LATER they were still talking about Josie's new employee over dinner in their favorite restaurant—not that the discussion had changed since the topic was introduced. Sam repeated his opinion that Josie could face—and lose—a large discrimination lawsuit if she refused to hire someone on the basis of their sex. By the time Josie's fried shrimp appetizer had been demolished, she had come to accept the fact that there was no way around it: Island Contracting was about to hire a male employee Josie didn't know.

"I'll bet he's going to cause all sorts of problems," she sighed, pouring tartar sauce on the two crab cakes the waiter had just placed before her. "We've all always gotten along great. Dropping a preening single man into the mix . . . well it's going to be a big problem."

Sam chuckled. "You sound just like some older male partners of the firm I worked for in the seventies when the first women lawyers were hired."

"That's different!" she protested, her mouth full of crab.

"Not really."

"It was! It is! Especially in the construction industry!

Do you know the percentage of women in my business?"

"No, but . . ."

"Actually, neither do I, but I'm sure Nic can tell you all about it. The point is that Island Contracting's hiring policy has gone just a little way toward leveling the playing field, toward giving women an equal chance in a business where the only thing that should matter is that a worker can do the work, not what sex they happen to be."

"I think you may be arguing against yourself," Sam said gently, using his fork to stab one of the grilled shrimp atop his Caesar salad.

"But you know what I'm trying to say."

"I do, and I've appreciated the opportunities you've provided by hiring women in a business generally not thought of as appropriate for them. But the law is the law. You can't tell this man that he doesn't have a job because he's the wrong sex." He put the shrimp in his mouth and chewed thoughtfully. "How did Nic end up offering this guy a job, anyway? I would have thought that was the last thing in the world she would do."

"She thought he was a woman."

"I gather they haven't met."

"They have now, but they hadn't when she offered him the job." Josie put down her fork and concentrated on her explanation. "See, Nic ran into an old friend at the convention, a carpenter named Vicki. They got to talking and Nic told Vicki about Island Contracting, and ended up suggesting Vicki apply for a job. Vicki said fine, and asked if Island Contracting was interested in hiring an electrician she knew. Well, Nic couldn't ignore that. We've been looking for competent electricians since Island Electric shut down."

Sam nodded.

"And, anyway, this Vicki said the electrician's name is Leslie."

"More men are named Leslie than women, in my experience at least."

Josie didn't argue. "But the real problem is that Nic got the impression that Vicki and Leslie were involved romantically."

"But . . ."

"And she had always assumed that Vicki was a lesbian."

"Apparently that's not true?"

"Apparently not. She's involved with Leslie."

"Then, if Leslie is taken, maybe there won't be any problems."

"You may be right—and the entire crew knows each other."

"Really?"

"Yeah. Leslie and Vicki asked if there was a job for their friend, a carpenter named Mary Ann."

"Have you hired her too?"

"Yes. In fact I've turned in their personnel information to my insurance company and they're all here on the island looking for apartments . . ."

"But you haven't met them?"

"No, but I've only hired them provisionally; if there are any problems, out they go."

"Leaving you without a crew right at the beginning of the summer," Sam reminded her.

"I know, but I don't have a whole lot of options this year. I made some calls the day before yesterday and you were right. No one seems to be available. The formation of two new contracting companies on the island has created a real shortage of workers."

"Josie, this summer is going to be extra busy for you— you're going to be planning our wedding as well as working."

"And Tyler. Don't forget Tyler."

"Oh, it's impossible to forget Tyler even when he's five hundred miles away at school."

Josie put down her fork, half of her crab cakes untouched. "It's been years since Tyler spent a summer on the island."

"And you've always missed him terribly."

"I did, of course, but . . . well, I always thought he was better off at camp or school, that he should be learning things and keeping busy and . . . becoming independent. Growing up."

"All of which he has done very nicely. You know Tyler loves the island. He wants to spend more time here before he goes off to college. And he'll be busy. Working for the only company that creates publicity materials for most of the island businesses, beginning research for his senior project, and taking a class online, he probably won't have a moment to spare. It's not as though he's going to be sleeping late and lounging around the house."

"I know. Tyler has a lot of energy and I want to be with him." She grimaced and picked up her fork. "I guess I'm just not used to being a full-time mother anymore."

"You and Tyler may not have been living together twenty-four/seven, but you've been a full-time mother to him no matter where he is or what he's been doing."

Josie smiled. "It's nice of you to say so. I guess I'm just afraid he'll be bored staying here this summer."

"Tyler is incapable of being bored, and you are changing the subject so you don't have to figure out what you're going to do if this new crew doesn't work out."

"There's no way I can figure that out ahead of time. If it doesn't work, I'll have to find new people and there's no telling who might be available," she added, knowing perfectly well who would be available late in the season: the carpenters, electricians, and plumbers no one wanted to hire—usually for good reasons.

"There is one personnel decision we could make right now," Sam suggested quietly.

"What?" Josie asked, surprised. Sam didn't interfere in Island Contracting business unless she asked for help, and he was usually reluctant to get involved even then.

"We could ask Basil to cater our wedding reception. Even if you decide against a big wedding, we owe it to our friends to have a party to celebrate our union. If Basil's free and says yes, it's one less thing to worry about. One less decision to make later," he added gently.

"I guess that's okay. Do you think he'll make those little lobster quiches?"

"I'm sure he'll make anything you ask him to make."

Josie finished off the last of her dinner, pushed back from the table, and yawned. "I'm exhausted. I think I'd better head home and get to bed. I have to be up early tomorrow. There was a message from the insurance company on my machine this afternoon. No one answered at the office when I called back, but I need to touch base with my agent. We can't get down to work until I have everyone included on my insurance policy, so I sure hope there aren't any problems."

"No dessert?"

She hesitated. Dessert was her favorite course. "I wonder what sort of pie's on the menu tonight . . ."

A young waitress appeared at their table in time to hear her question. "Raspberry cream, Dutch apple, and Shaker lemon slice. It's made with slices of fresh lemons, nothing like lemon meringue, and it's become a real favorite in the past few weeks when it's on the menu."

"Could I have a slice of the lemon—no, two slices; I'll bring one home to Tyler—to go?" Josie asked.

"Don't see why not. Would you like one too?" she asked Sam.

"I think I'll just take the check. An early night sounds like a good idea. Mother's due on the island sometime tomorrow and I'd like to straighten up the house a bit before she arrives."

"Why bother? She'd love to do it for you."

"I know. And I know if I don't do some cleaning before she comes, I'll spend the next few weeks looking for things she's 'put away.' "

"I suppose Carol's going to want to be involved in any wedding plans."

"I can't imagine anything else, but Mother knows this is our wedding. She'll leave the decisions up to us."

Josie wasn't sure how true that was, but the pie had arrived, two extra-large slices packed up in Styrofoam containers, and as soon as Sam signed the credit card receipt, she was ready to hit the road.

As Sam had said, Tyler wasn't hanging around the house watching television. A note taped to her apartment door informed Josie that her son was at a beach party given by old family friends and would be home sometime around midnight. Josie sat down on the couch and, discovering the remote control beneath a pile of her son's computer magazines, flipped on the television. In a few minutes she was chuckling over a rerun of *Frasier*. By the time the show ended, she had finished both pieces of pie. She was throwing away the evidence of her gluttony when she noticed the light flashing on her answering machine.

The message was from her insurance agent, asking her to call him at home if it "wasn't too late" when she got his message. Josie frowned. What was too late for one person was the shank of the evening to another, but her agent had never before called her at home. That, combined with the fact that this was the second call today, worried Josie enough for her to decide that it very definitely wasn't too late. She reached for the phone.

It wasn't good news and it was delivered rather abruptly by her agent, who explained that he didn't mind her calling—it was just that he had been in the shower. When Josie hung up a few minutes later, she knew she had a problem. Leslie Coyne was uninsurable.

There are people who eat when they're worried and those who don't. Josie could never understand the latter group. She headed straight for her freezer where she expected to find a pint or two of Ben and Jerry's finest.

Unfortunately Tyler had gotten there first. Her small freezer was empty except for three ice cube trays, a frost-covered Weight Watchers mac and cheese meal, and a bag of peas so old Josie couldn't be sure that they hadn't been in the freezer when she rented the apartment. She closed one door and opened the other. The refrigerator wasn't much better. And there was no milk—a necessity for a teenage boy who could easily empty two boxes of cereal in twenty-four hours. She sighed and reached for her purse. A trip to the twenty-four-hour Wawa was in order.

Less than fifteen blocks away from her apartment, the convenience store marked the beginning of the small town at the southern end of the island. As usual at this time of day, the parking lot was busy with customers coming and going, buying the last six-pack of the day, or picking up Rice Krispies for tomorrow's breakfast. Josie noticed Leslie Coyne driving off as she pulled into a parking spot, hopped out of her truck, and hurried into the crowded store, determined to quickly complete her errand. Unfortunately the woman at the head of the check-out line had misplaced her credit card. By the time the sliver of platinum plastic had been discovered tucked in a side pocket of her Coach carry-all, Josie was about to scream with frustration.

And that was before she left the store and found her son sitting in the police cruiser parked out front.

"Tyler!"

"Mom!"

"What's going on? I thought you were going to a beach party."

Officer Trish Petric answered Josie's question. "We're just talking, Ms. Pigeon. That's all that's going on here. Your son and I were having a little chat. And now I think it's time he went home. I have to finish my patrol." And much to Josie's amazement, her son—with a sheepish expression she had never before seen on his face—got out of the car and, thrusting his hands in his jeans pockets, stared at the ground.

"Get in the truck and we'll go home," Josie said.

"I rode my bike here."

"Toss it in the back."

"I'd rather ride home . . . it won't take more than five minutes," he added. Tyler hopped on his bike and had taken off in the other direction before his mother could protest.

She bit her bottom lip. She could use those five minutes to think of something to say to him . . . maybe. What did any mother say to her child after discovering him "chatting" with the local police? What could Tyler have done? Underage drinking, illegal drugs, and shoplifting all came to mind immediately, but none of those things sounded like her son. But wasn't the family frequently the last to know when teenagers had serious problems? Could Tyler be suffering from a serious addiction and she hadn't even had an inkling of the problem? She drove home, her imagination active. By the time Tyler walked into their apartment, she had envisioned him homeless on the streets of a big impersonal city after a long series of unsuccessful stints in various treatment centers. So vivid was her vision that she was almost shocked by his happy, wholesome demeanor as he greeted his cat.

"Hi there, Urch, time for bed," he announced, lifting his small Burmese cat high in the air.

"Why were you talking to that police officer?" Josie asked, knowing immediately that she sounded rather ridiculous.

"Officer Petric had some questions for me, about some of the kids on the island. Nothing serious," he added, heading, as he usually did, for the refrigerator. "Anything to eat in here? I'm starving."

Josie smiled. That was her Tyler—always hungry. And he was exactly the right person for Officer Petric to question about the other teenagers. Tyler knew and was liked by everyone. "There's cereal, and I just bought milk. And I hid a bag of Mint Milanos in the cupboard over the refrigerator," she added, smiling now that she no longer had to worry.

"Thanks, Ma. I've been waiting to get my hands on those cookies," Tyler said, reaching for the bag.

Josie grinned at him. "I'm going to head off to bed. Tomorrow is going to be a long day for me. What are you doing?"

"Working, working, working. You know me—nose to the grindstone," he said. His reply was rather muffled as his mouth was full of cookies.

"Sam's mother is coming to the island tomorrow. Do you want to join us for dinner?"

"Yeah, cool. I don't want to miss any of Carol's cooking."

"I'll call and let you know what time. Make sure your cell phone is charged, okay?"

"My cell's always charged—you're the one who forgets to charge your phone, Ma."

"Well, we'll see you at dinner then."

Josie was in the shower before she realized that Tyler could have used the five minutes it took to ride his bike home to decide what excuse he would offer for being discovered in the patrol car "chatting" with Trish Petric, that he hadn't mentioned why he wasn't at the beach party, and that he had managed to go to bed without explaining anything about his evening.

It took her longer than usual to fall asleep.

FOUR

LIVING IN A resort community has its own special set of problems. People on vacation are relaxed. Josie was always in a rush, trying to get jobs done on time, before the season ended, before the autumn storms arrived. People on vacation spend money impulsively. Josie was constantly worried about where each dollar went, both in her private life and on Island Contracting's books. And people on vacation sleep late. Josie's alarm went off at 5:30. Today, after hours of tossing about on sheets that desperately needed to spend some time in a washing machine, it was almost a relief to get up and get going.

Josie's morning routine was more "no maintenance" than "low maintenance," and she was out the door less than five minutes after setting her feet on the floor. Driving to her office, she stopped worrying about Tyler and focused on work. First problem: insurance. Second problem: a new and unknown crew. Third problem: well, she wasn't sure what the third problem was, but she suspected she would know in a few hours.

Island Contracting's office was a converted fishing shack which hung over the bay dividing the island from the mainland. Remodeled by Noel Roberts, former owner of the company and Josie's mentor, it was both charming and practical. Josie dedicated as much of her free time as was necessary to maintaining it, and the first rays of daylight bounced off paint applied only the month before. Making a mental note to water the nasturtium seedlings beginning to emerge from the soil in the window boxes, she unlocked the front door, switched on the overhead light, and headed straight for the coffee maker.

A caramel-colored tabby kitten, dozing on the counter, lifted her head off a packet of coffee filters and meowed a greeting.

"Coffee for me, then kitten chow for you," Josie promised, reaching for a bag of ground beans.

In minutes the scent of freshly brewed coffee mingled with the ever-present aroma of tidal mud, and the kitten, happily fed, was playing with a brilliant red crab shell on the floor while Josie worked at her computer.

Her insurance agent had sent a long e-mail explaining that Leslie Coyne could not be covered by Island Contracting's insurance policy. Josie dutifully printed out all the information and then poured her first mug of coffee of the day. She had no idea what she was going to do. According to the man she had been buying insurance from for almost a decade, Leslie Coyne was uninsurable because he had "a previous medical condition," although the agent couldn't say more because medical information is confidential. But she was assured that once the condition cleared up—and remained cleared up for a certain, unspecified number of years—he would be eligible for health insurance again, at a premium.

Her coffee grew cold as she considered the situation. She couldn't afford the liability of an uninsured worker. But if Leslie left, would Vickie leave as well? She also couldn't afford to be two workers short at the beginning of the season and she had no idea how, or if, she could replace them. Damn! She got up and stomped out onto the deck overhanging the bay behind her office. The sun was sparkling off the water. A lone kayaker paddled by and smiled up at her. Josie waved and plunked herself down on one of the ragged captain's chairs to think.

She was still thinking when she realized she was no longer alone.

"Hi . . . you didn't hear me come in, did you?" Leslie Coyne was standing in the open doorway; the kitten, dwarfed by his huge biceps, was nestled in his arms.

"No. But I was thinking about you."

"Shit. I guess you've heard from your insurance company."

"How did you know?"

He shrugged. "It happens. Usually sooner rather than later. But you don't have to worry. I don't mind working without insurance."

"But you can't do that! What if you get hurt?"

"I'll be careful. I won't."

Josie stood up. "You don't know what might happen. And . . ."

"And you're afraid I'll get hurt and sue your company."

Actually, Josie hadn't gotten any further than Leslie getting hurt in her thinking. "I . . . would you sue Island Contracting?"

"Of course not. I'd never get another job if it got out that I had sued my last employer. And I'd be happy to sign something. You know, a statement that I won't sue. I've worked for other companies that were content to leave it at that."

Josie thought for a minute. "Why can't you get health insurance?" she finally asked. "What's wrong with you—

if you don't mind my asking," she added, perhaps a bit late.

"Multiple sclerosis. The first symptoms appeared about five years ago."

"But insurance companies can't just drop your coverage because you become ill! One of my carpenters had cancer and she was covered."

"I was too—at first. But then I became too ill to work. I went on disability for almost a year. It was barely enough money to survive on despite help from my family and friends. If I hadn't used my ingenuity, I would have starved. But then I was lucky enough to go into remission so I could return to work, only to discover that I couldn't get insurance. It might be a different situation if I had one of those jobs you stay in forever, but I've always moved around from job to job. You know how it is in our business. So it's been easy for insurance companies to deny me coverage when I—or the company I work for—apply for it."

"But isn't there anything you can do?"

"In some states I could apply for Medicaid, but then I couldn't work, and I like to work and I like to make money. So I have little choice but to work without insurance and make sure nothing happens to me."

"I never knew anything like that could happen."

"No one does, until it happens to them or someone they know." Leslie was quiet for a moment. "So, do I have the job or don't I?"

Josie didn't see how she could say anything other than, "Of course you do."

"I'd be happy to sign a document promising not to sue . . ."

Josie stood up. "That won't be necessary," she said. "I

trust you. You trust me. That's the way Island Contracting has always worked."

"Thank you. Thanks a million," Leslie said, grabbing her hand and shaking it energetically.

"I'd better finish up here. We're all due on site in less than an hour," Josie reminded him.

"I'll pick up Vicki and we'll be there on time—or early even!" he added, dashing off.

Alone on the deck, Josie stared down at the water. She had just made a huge mistake and she had known it as soon as she had done it. She didn't know Leslie and had no reason to trust him. If Sam found out, he'd go nuts. She might even be risking the future of Island Contracting—and for a man! It was a lousy way to begin a job. Josie finished up at the office and drove over to the Higgins's house feeling less than her normal enthusiasm at the beginning of a new project.

A good-looking young man was standing on the porch, hands stuffed into the pockets of his chinos, with what looked like a cashmere sweater carefully tied around his neck. Josie wondered what a vacationer was doing up and about so early, and on the Higgins's property. She parked her truck by the curb, got out, and started up the sidewalk to the house, calling out a greeting.

"Hi yourself," the stranger replied, smiling. "You must be Josie Pigeon."

"I am. Who are you?"

"Christopher Higgins. I'm your architect."

"You're . . . are you old enough to be an architect?" The words were out of her mouth before she realized just how rude she sounded. "I mean, you don't look much older than my son. And he's just seventeen," she added, realizing she was making things worse.

"I'll be twenty-one in July. This will be my first professional job," Christopher Higgins admitted, smiling proudly. "I was thrilled when Grandfather bought this place and suggested I draw up plans to remodel it."

"Seymour Higgins is your grandfather?" Josie asked.

"Yes. Cool, isn't it?"

"Yeah, cool," she replied unenthusiastically. Just what she needed—an inexperienced architect.

"I can't wait for your crew to get started." Christopher Higgins appeared to hesitate. "There are a few last-minute changes that I wanted to talk over with you."

"Changes?"

"A few very minor changes." He picked up an elegant and expensive-looking calfskin briefcase from the floor. "I have the drawings here, if you have a few moments to take a look."

"I . . ."

"I'm going to show them to my grandparents as soon as we go over them," he added.

At least he was giving her an opportunity to see them first. "Sure," she said trying to sound enthusiastic. "Let's go inside."

"Great. I think you're really going to be interested in this. I'm proposing some really innovative concepts."

To Josie, *innovative* sounded like it meant *expensive*. She had signed a contract with Seymour Higgins and they had agreed on a price. Changes would be made throughout the project—there always were—but making changes before the demolition even began made Josie nervous.

"And some of my ideas are real money savers. Grandfather and Grandmother will really like that!"

"But I thought they were rich. I mean . . ."

"Oh, they are, but Grandfather says only fools don't

like bargains, and Grandmother clips the coupons in the paper every Sunday and insists that her housekeeper use them when she shops. They're both going to appreciate all the money we're going to save them."

Josie wasn't quite so sure about that "we" in his statement, but she didn't feel the need to share this with him. "Let's look at those plans. My crew is going to be here to start demolition in a few minutes."

He hesitated a moment on the door step. "I pulled a few things I thought Grandmother and Grandfather might want to save—some pieces of furniture—and put them in the garage. I hope you don't mind."

"No problem." In fact, it was the first thing that morning that wasn't a problem. After her conversation with Sam the day before, she was going to insist that her crew empty the house and carefully store the contents.

Christopher opened the door for Josie and she walked into the house.

Josie realized immediately that Christopher's idea of "a few things" was different than hers: her immediate impression was that the house had been stripped of almost all the sixties touches that Sam had waxed so enthusiastically over the previous day. She smiled. He had just saved her and her crew a few hours of tedious work. Now they could immediately get busy with crowbars and sledge hammers.

Just as soon as she looked at Christopher's ideas . . .

FIVE

MONTHS LATER, JOSIE was to realize how lucky it was that she had been so busy that day; otherwise she might have taken the time to count all the things going wrong with the Bride's Secret Bed and Breakfast project, and the resulting list would certainly have been a daunting one.

Christopher was a self-confident young man, happy to pass the spare time that Josie certainly didn't have talking about himself. He revealed the name of his girl-friend; he mentioned where he was going to college; he apparently thought nothing of explaining that this project was his first architectural job. It wasn't actually a professional job, he explained. His grandparents weren't paying him for his work, but, he added, at least he would get college credit.

Josie had been forced to interrupt at that point. "You mean you're in graduate school?" she asked, hoping for a positive answer.

"No, but I'll be a senior next year. In fact, this house is my senior thesis project. This should be an easy year for me, don't you think? I mean, most of my work will be done this summer."

"Let me get this straight. You haven't graduated from

college. You've never had a professional architectural job in your life. This will be the first time anyone has ever built anything using plans you've drawn?"

"Yeah, it's really neat of Grandfather and Grandmother to trust me, don't you think?"

"Yeah, really neat," Josie lied, wondering what was wrong with these people. Why couldn't they just hang their grandkid's artwork on their refrigerator like everyone else in the country?

"And I've come up with an innovative concept that will blow away my professors. You could be starting on a project that will turn up in *Architectural Digest*."

Or one that will destroy Island Contracting's reputation. Josie sighed and made a suggestion. "Why don't we lay your plans out on the counter in the kitchen, and you can explain everything to me. In detail."

It took over an hour, during which time her crew arrived and was instructed to finish removing furniture from the upper floors of the house, and to store everything except broken-down wicker in the garage. Christopher explained, drew diagrams in the dust on the countertop, waved his arms around in circles to demonstrate the scope of his vision, and finally got down to brass tacks and explained an alternative solar energy system that he claimed to have designed. It was a piece of this, a bit of that, and it might actually save his grandparents money—if they lived sixty more years and the sun decided to shine at least twenty hours a day for each and every one of those years. Josie had no choice but to try to talk the young man out of his idea.

"It's not that this isn't interesting—it is," she lied. "But this is all custom work, and I'm honestly not sure Island Contracting has the expertise needed to do it. We could find a specialist if you and your grandparents decide to go solar. There are companies doing wonderful, innovative work on solar energy, but most of their installations work better on new homes. Retrofitting can be very complex and incredibly expensive. And this island isn't exactly situated in the Sun Belt, you know," she added gently. Christopher looked crushed. If his ideas weren't threatening to screw up her project, she would feel some sympathy for him.

He seemed to take her suggestion seriously. "What about wind power? We're on the ocean. There are winds—the prevailing westerlies . . ." he finished somewhat less confidently.

"We're on the east coast. The prevailing westerlies come from the west, don't they?" Josie wasn't absolutely sure of her facts here, but she did remember quizzing Tyler about wind currents for a test when he was in fourth grade.

"I . . . yeah, I guess."

"And I don't think the island's planning commission would give you permission to erect windmills on the property," Josie said.

"Yeah. Well, I thought of that, of course." Christopher stared down at the blueprints and chewed on his top lip.

"I noticed that you did a real nice job placing skylights in the mansard roof . . ." Josie began, now truly feeling sorry for him.

"And they open—they will help cool the house in the evening," he explained a bit more enthusiastically. "Ventilation can be a real problem in these old houses."

"And you've located two heavy-duty exhaust fans in the attic as well."

"Yeah, I wanted to keep the symmetry of the home intact. Besides, two fans will move twice as much air as one."

"That's an excellent idea. Efficient, inexpensive, unobtrusive," Josie said. She was beginning to wonder if her job really was to encourage this young man rather than getting to work with her crew.

"And I've been thinking about the stained glass windows at the top of the attic stairs."

"You're going to remove them? Have you checked with your grandparents about that?" Actually, Josie thought they were ugly, but she knew lots of people admired that type of window, even though they blocked the view and certainly didn't improve ventilation.

"No, my Grandmother particularly mentioned remembering those windows from her youth, but I know of a company that removes the glass, resets it in frames that can be pivoted so they open and close, and then replaces them in the wall. They look exactly the same, but of course they're much more functional."

"Who removes them and who installs them after they're altered?" Josie asked. She didn't know this company, and she didn't want Island Contracting to end up responsible for someone else's shoddy work.

"They do. It's all guaranteed, too. I'll give you the company's number if you would like to check them out."

She nodded. "Definitely."

"They'll be here at the end of the week—unless you want me to call and reschedule," he added. "I think . . . I'm sure I can convince them to do that if it's necessary."

Josie considered her answer for a bit before speaking. "No, the end of the week will be fine, but you need to check these things out with me before scheduling anything else. My ladies . . ." She stopped, realizing she could no long use this term when talking about her crew. "My crew can't do two things at once. And it's easier for us and safer for delicate windows and woodwork to remain at the place where they're fashioned until we're ready to install them, rather than sitting on the worksite for any length of time. That's why we always specify delivery dates when we order replacement windows and the like."

He nodded. "I'd never thought about it like that."

Josie sighed. Of course he hadn't. He had probably been busy figuring out how to buy beer without an ID. "Look, I'm sorry to dash off, but I need to get to work with my crew."

Christopher took the hint. "Then I'll leave you alone. I just want to check out where the drain lines from the bathrooms meet on the second floor. It would be nice to follow the same path for the new ones . . . right?" He looked to her for confirmation.

She smiled. "Right!" Christopher was a quick learner. If she could teach him to check out all the details with her, this could turn out to be an easy project.

That optimistic thought evaporated before she left the kitchen and set her foot on the bottom step. A loud noise, something crashing to the floor no doubt, and certainly not unusual on a worksite, sent her clomping up the stairs two at a time. What if Leslie had been hurt?

She arrived on the landing to discover her entire crew laughing loudly. Leslie was sprawled on the floor, a large sledgehammer clasped to his bare chest. Nic was leaning against the wall, Vicki at her side, both in need of support as they howled. Mary Ann, laughing as well, stood squarely in the center of the room, supporting the ceiling over her head. Josie ran over to help out.

"What happened?" Josie asked as she and Mary Ann lowered the wallboard to the floor.

Vicki stopped laughing long enough to explain. "Leslie gave the wall a smack and the ceiling fell down."

"And Mary Ann caught it," Nic added. "The whole thing."

Apparently you had to be there, Josie decided. To be sure, she was relieved that no one had been hurt, but she was also smiling because her crew was getting along so well on their first day together. "We'll have to be more careful. It looks as though whoever divided up the rooms used the cheapest materials and didn't know a whole lot about standard construction techniques."

Nic was examining the wall board. "Yeah, not a whole lot of nails in this thing. Looks like the tear down will be easy."

"I don't know," Leslie said, getting up from the floor and walking over to a wall socket. "Look at this . . . it wasn't even grounded properly. The third wire's just hanging. We better be careful."

"Don't tell me the only man on the crew is afraid of a little electric shock," Mary Ann said.

Josie waited to see how Leslie responded to Mary Ann's teasing. He brushed his hair back off his forehead, his hand leaving a trail of dirt, and looked over the entire group before answering. "I've been shocked more times than I can count, but I've never been in the middle of a house on fire—and that's what we need to worry about. I'm strong, but I don't think I can carry all four of you out of a burning building at the same time." He smiled, revealing even white teeth. "Unless, of course, one of you ladies would like to carry me."

"In your dreams," Nic said.

"Not a chance," Mary Ann added.

Vicki just laughed. "I guess my fiancé has delusions of grandeur."

"Your fiancé? I thought you were . . . well, I thought you were just dating," Josie said, both relieved at how well Leslie took the women's teasing and surprised by Vicki's statement.

"So did I," Nic said.

"We were, but . . ." Vicki looked over at Leslie and smiled. "We've become more than that in the time we've been together."

"You always were a fast worker," Mary Ann said to Leslie.

"How long have you known Leslie?" Nic asked her.

"Oh, years. I think we first met on a job about two years ago, right Les?" Mary Ann replied.

"I didn't know that." Nic spoke slowly.

"It doesn't really matter, does it?" Leslie asked, his charming smile reappearing on his face.

"It does to me," Nic answered. "That's not what I thought, or what I told Josie. I misrepresented you."

"But it's like Leslie said," Vicki pointed out. "It doesn't really matter."

"It does to me. You're here on the island because I found jobs for you at Island Contracting. I'm responsible . . ."

"No, you're not," Josie said. "I am. And, as of this moment, I'm happy with the work you're all doing. But this is a small crew on a big job—it's essential that we all get along. It's your job to see that you get along. And I expect that you'll all do just that.

"Now, I don't know about you all, but I'm hungry. Time for lunch." She had made her point. She got up and headed for the door. "My treat," she called back over her shoulder. "I assume we can all agree on that."

SIX

ISLAND CONTRACTING HIRED new workers each season. This was partially determined by the company's location, as there weren't many carpenters, plumbers, and electricians living full time in this expensive beach community. And while there was always work available during the summer, the winter months were slow. But for many years Josie had worked with one other woman. Betty Jacobs, currently mother and East Side matron, had been Betty Patrick, carpenter and sexy island native for years before her marriage to one of Sam's best friends. Josie frequently missed her friend, but never as much as she did at this moment. She desperately needed someone to talk to. And Sam, she knew, was not that someone.

Unfortunately, he was standing at the back of the line of customers in front of the counter as she entered the Italian deli at the north end of the island. His smile indicated that he didn't share her reluctance to see him.

"Josie! What are you doing here? You usually don't take a break on the first day of a new job." He planted a kiss on top of her red mop.

"I'm treating my crew to lunch. Most of them are new to the island and don't know the best places to eat yet.

43

But what are you doing here? You don't usually go in for this type of food," she added, peering over the counter as a huge, oily, Italian roll was stuffed with ham, cheese, and salami before being cut in half and rolled in wax paper.

"Mother says the imported prosciutto here is as good as Dean and Deluca sells. She wants to serve it with figs for a first course tonight—it's a great combination—better than with melon, I think. So if you want some, you'd better be on time for dinner."

Josie bent her lips into something resembling a smile, but not quite enough like a smile to fool Sam.

"What's wrong? Anything I can do? Isn't the new crew working out?" His own smile had been replaced with an expression of concern.

She made a better effort. "Nothing. I was up early doing paperwork . . . and you know how I hate paperwork."

He did. "I could take that particular burden off you, you know."

He had made this offer before. Josie would have loved someone else to take over Island Contracting's paperwork, and she would allow that to happen just as soon as she got everything in order so she didn't risk dying of embarrassment over the state it was in. She figured that would happen sometime in 2020—if she was exceptionally diligent. "I know, and I may take you up on that sometime. You're next," she pointed out, as the man in front of Sam walked off with his bag of hoagies.

Sam placed his order and turned back to Josie. "Too bad you have to eat with your crew—it's a gorgeous day. Perfect for a picnic on the beach."

Josie pursed her lips. "I can't . . . I mean, I really do have to eat with my crew. We have a lot to discuss."

"I know. Perhaps when we're married. . . ."

"I think that's your Mom's ham," Josie interrupted. "Six double Italians—no peppers on two," she told the man behind the counter. "And I'll take two six packs of Diet Coke as well." She turned back to Sam.

"How is your mother doing?" she asked, mainly to be polite.

"She's fine, but I think I should warn you. She's sort of enthusiastic about our wedding . . ."

"That doesn't surprise me."

"And you know how Mother gets when she's enthusiastic."

Josie nodded. "Right over the top."

"She has everything planned right down to the favors for the guests."

"Favors?"

"Small candles shaped like wedding cakes. Actually, they're sort of charming."

They sounded anything but charming to Josie. "Did she bring them with her?"

"Just samples." He hesitated. "She pointed out that it's easier to get things in New York City than here. Which is true, of course. Josie . . . I think she's going to talk to you about your wedding dress tonight. Mother says most brides in the city order their gown months ahead of time, and she's worried that you won't be able to find one you like this close to the wedding."

Josie could only sigh.

"She just wants everything to be perfect for you," he added.

"I know. I really do know that, Sam. I just . . . I can't deal with that right this moment. This project . . ."

"Of course. Don't worry about a thing. I'll remind Mother that you're a working woman and you can't spend every minute of the day worrying about our wedding. I'm sure she'll understand."

Josie wasn't so sure, but her order was ready, so she paid the bill and allowed Sam to help her carry everything to her truck.

"You know how much I love you, Josie," he said, leaning through the open window.

She looked into his blue eyes and she knew. "I do. I really do."

"So you don't have to worry about a thing. We'll have the wedding you want and it will be perfect."

"I just hope we make it though the planning phase without offending every single one of our friends and relatives."

"Yeah. Well, they'll get over it. Oh, Mother wanted me to find out if Tyler is coming to dinner tonight."

"Definitely. But you know he eats everything. She doesn't have to make special plans for him."

"I think she was deciding whether to have pound cake and fruit for dessert or pound cake and ice cream. She assumed Tyler would prefer the ice cream."

"Definitely," Josie said, not bothering to add that she would as well. "Sam, last night Tyler . . ."

Sam's cell phone trilled the first few stanzas of Mozart's "A Little Night Music" and he answered before she could continue. Josie didn't have to hear more than his side of the conversation to realize there was trouble at the store. "I've got to run," he told her—not a surprise since she had just listened to him tell the person on the other end of the line that he would be there immediately. "That new cop gave one of my regular delivery men a ticket, and he's threatening to stop making deliveries to the island."

"Most delivery men know not to speed," Josie said.

"This was a parking ticket. Apparently the rear wheels of his truck were outside of the line demarcating the loading zone."

"There's something wrong with that woman. Last night . . ."

"Josie, I really have to run. Dinner's at seven tonight."

"I'll call if I'm going to be late," she said, but Sam was already shifting his MGB into gear. He roared off down the street, and she hoped Officer Petric wasn't patrolling the ten or so blocks between the deli and Sam's store.

She wasn't, because she was manning a speed trap right around the corner from the deli—a speed trap Josie drove right into. She pulled over and waited for Officer Petric to stroll up to her truck.

"Ms. Pigeon, are you aware that you were going forty-five in a twenty-five-mile-per-hour zone?"

"Not really. You see, my speedometer hasn't been working, but I usually drive under the island speed limit. I've lived here for a long time. I'm used to it," Josie continued, although she was aware of the fact that she didn't have Officer Petric's attention.

"When I took this job, I was warned that some of the natives might expect special attention, but . . ."

"Look, I'm not a native. I wasn't born here. And I certainly don't make a habit of speeding. And . . . are you writing me a speeding ticket?"

"No. I'm just giving you a verbal warning. But I can't ignore that expired inspection sticker," she added, ripping a sheet of paper off her pad and passing it to Josie. "You'll see there's a court date and time. Be there." And, without giving Josie time to say anything (which might have been lucky, considering what Josie was about to say), the woman spun on her heels and returned to her cruiser. Josie turned the key in the ignition, put the truck in gear, and drove off. She was furious, and her face was nearly the color of her red hair.

She drove the fifty or so blocks back to the work site as slowly as possible. A couple of joggers passed her, chatting and laughing. Bicycles whizzed by. A woman pushing a baby in a stroller very nearly kept pace. And Officer Trish Petric stayed right on her tail.

By the time Josie arrived at her destination, she was so upset that she didn't even wonder why her entire crew was sitting on the front porch doing nothing instead of being inside ripping down walls. She tucked the ticket in the breast pocket of her overalls, grabbed the now-dripping bag of hoagies, and started toward the house to join her crew.

She was surprised when the policewoman pulled over to the curb behind her truck. Didn't this woman have anything to do other than hassle Josie and those she cared about? But she was even more surprised when her crew jumped down off the porch and met her halfway to the house.

"Hey, I know you've all been working hard, but we just took a coffee break less than an hour ago," Josie said, handing the bag of sandwiches to Leslie. She looked over her shoulder. Officer Petric was sitting in the cruiser staring up at the house. "There's Diet Coke in the truck," she continued. At least she wouldn't get a ticket for abusing her workers or some other trumped up charge.

"I'll get the Coke," Vicki offered.

"We should eat on the porch," Mary Ann said.

"It would be cooler inside . . ." Josie began.

"We should eat on the porch," Nic said, glancing at the police car and then back to Josie.

Josie decided to exert some authority. "I think . . ."

"It's okay," Mary Ann interrupted. "The cop is leaving."

"Let's all go inside," Leslie said.

Josie was beginning to feel as though no one was listening to her, and she didn't like the feeling. "I think . . ."

"There's a body upstairs," Nic interrupted again. "A dead body."

Josie looked over her shoulder.

"Don't worry," Leslie said. "We waited until she was gone to say anything."

Well, Josie thought, at least she had hired a smart crew.

SEVEN

WHERE DID YOU *find it? Do you know who it is?* These and about a million other questions occurred to Josie as she followed her crew back into the house, but no one said anything until the front doors were closed and they could no longer be heard by anyone on the street. Then she couldn't wait any longer.

"Where did you find it? Do you know who it is? Is it a woman or a man? How did he . . . or she die? Who found . . ."

"We'll show you," Mary Ann spoke up. "She's upstairs."

"Les knocked down the wall and . . . well, and there she was . . . and there she is." Vicki, not surprisingly, sounded upset.

"Where?"

"Behind the linen closet at the end of the hall on the second floor." Leslie answered.

"What are we going to do?" Vicki asked.

Josie was honest. "I don't know."

"I guess just walling her back up is out of the question," Leslie said, and Josie thought she detected a bit of wishful thinking.

"Yes, it certainly is . . ."

They had arrived at the top of the stairs and Josie led the way down the hallway toward what looked like a thick roll of drop cloths. Only when they were closer did she realize that there were feet protruding from one end—feet wearing socks woven with a design of flamingos and encased in bright pink Keds.

Josie knelt down and peered into the opposite end of the roll. Long blond hair and the top of a pair of sequin-adorned sunglasses were all she could make out in one quick look, and one quick look was all she could stand.

"Crap." She leaned back on her heels and repeated the word. "Crap."

"What are we going to do?" Vicki asked.

"We have to call the police, don't we?" Mary Ann said.

"Yeah, but how are we going to explain that we didn't speak up when Josie arrived here with that police escort?" Leslie asked.

"That might be a problem," Vicki agreed.

"I don't see why. We were in shock. Finding a dead body hidden behind a wall isn't something that happens every day. I don't think anyone can blame us for anything we did or didn't do," Mary Ann said.

"But . . ."

"Let's go downstairs." Josie interrupted.

"Do you think we should just leave her here?" Mary Ann asked.

Josie stood up. "She'll be fine here for the time being. And I don't know about you all, but I'll be more comfortable someplace else."

They all seemed to agree.

The bag of hoagies was waiting for them on a shelf in the foyer, but no one was particularly interested in lunch. Josie passed them out anyway. She had been through this before, and knew that keeping as normal a schedule as possible would help alleviate the stress. Besides, she was a person who needed to eat when she was nervous.

Apparently Leslie fell into that category as well, she thought, watching him rip open the wrapping and take a huge bite of his sandwich. Nic, Vicki, and Mary Ann didn't join the feast. Mary Ann sat down on the bottom step staring at her food without eating as much as a nibble. Nic didn't even bother to take the last sandwich; she just stood staring out the window to the street. Vicki took one bite, gagged, and rushed out into the backyard where, Josie assumed, she threw up in private.

"We have to call the police, but I think we should take a few minutes and talk first," Josie began. "You see, I've dealt with the police on this island for years and they're . . . well, they're incompetent at best."

"And at worst?" Leslie asked, his mouth full.

"I know this is going to sound odd, to say the least, but they hate me. You see, the permanent police force is made up of Mike Rodney Senior and Mike Rodney Junior. And Mike Rodney Junior is . . . was . . . well, we dated for a while. It didn't work out, and I stopped seeing him. He wasn't happy about that, and he and his father have been hassling me ever since." And the new officer on the island seemed to be following in that tradition, she added to herself.

"But this is murder, not a speeding ticket," Vicki said, reappearing in the room.

"How do you know she was murdered?" Nic asked, turning around.

"She didn't roll herself in those cloths and build a wall

to hide behind," Mary Ann pointed out. "I suppose she might have died of natural causes before being hidden, but I can't imagine why anyone would do something like that."

"We don't really know anything." Leslie said.

"We know we have to call the police soon, so let's not worry about what we don't know, and focus on what we do," Josie suggested. "Leslie was ripping down that wall, right?"

"Yes. Just Sheetrock on two-by-fours, it didn't take any time at all. But when the wall came down, she came with it," Vicki explained.

"She fell on top of the rubble," Mary Ann added. "So she must have been propped up inside the wall. You know, standing up."

"Why?"

"Because if she had been lying on the floor, she wouldn't have fallen out like that," Mary Ann said. "I mean, she might have sort of rolled out, but she wouldn't have fallen over on top of the wallboard and stuff, would she?"

"No, I guess not. Look," Josie added, "I hate to do this, but I'm going to call the police and let them know what we've found. The longer we wait, the more explaining we're going to have to do."

"If they ask why we didn't call sooner, how are we going to explain the time lag?" Leslie asked.

Josie shrugged. "I don't think we have to. We can just say that we found the body when we were tearing down the wall. You four were together when the body was found and I was . . ." She remembered that Officer Petric had followed her here and would know her crew was waiting on the porch for her return. "Well, I was out picking up lunch, and you showed me as soon as I returned. If anyone asks about the time discrepancy, just let me handle it. Okay?"

"Sure," Nic agreed.

Mary Ann spoke up. "But we'll tell the truth, won't we? I don't believe in lying to the police."

"We won't lie. But remember what I told you. These police officers are not like the ones you might have run into other places," Josie warned.

Leslie held out his cell phone. "Do you want to call or shall I?"

"I will," Josie said. "I suppose I should use 911."

"Only if it's an emergency, Miss Pigeon."

She recognized that deep voice, and with a sigh, looked up and discovered Mike Rodney Senior, the island's chief of police, in the open doorway, leaning against the doorjamb. As usual, he was not smiling.

"I prefer to use *Ms.*, Chief Rodney."

"From what I hear, you're gonna be using Mrs. sometime at the end of summer. Guess I should offer my congratulations. Who woulda thought a carpenter like you would get herself a big-shot lawyer for a husband? Guess you have hidden talents, Miss Pigeon."

She knew she was being baited. And she knew she shouldn't rise to the bait. But she started to anyway. "I have . . ."

"We found a body," Mary Ann interrupted. "A dead body. Upstairs."

Chief Rodney slowly turned away from Josie. "What did you say?" He asked the question slowly, as though speaking to a backward child.

"There's a dead body upstairs." Nic spoke up. "A woman."

Chief Rodney shook his head. "What is it about you and dead bodies, Miss Pigeon?" he asked, apparently too surprised to take the opportunity to insult Josie.

Josie had no idea how to answer his question, so she ignored it. "She's in the hallway upstairs. She's the reason we were talking about calling the police when you arrived." She started toward the staircase. "I'll show you."

"No, you won't. I'll go up myself. You all can just wait down here." He yanked a cell phone from his pocket and punched in a number as he stomped up the risers.

No one said anything until he was out of sight. "God, you were telling the truth. He really doesn't like you," Mary Ann whispered.

Josie nodded. She looked over at Leslie and Vicki. Leslie was picking at a hangnail with an intent expression on his face. Vicki was staring at him as she chewed on her lower lip. Nic had turned her back on the room and was again gazing out the window to the street.

Josie could no longer hear the police chief's footsteps or his orders to whomever he had called. She leaned against the wall behind her. In a few minutes she would be involved in a murder investigation again, an investigation which might delay work on Island Contracting's biggest summer project. An investigation that would put her in frequent—possibly daily—contact with the island's police officers. An investigation that might even make it necessary to delay her wedding. Well, everything had its bright side, she decided, as Chief Rodney stomped back down the stairs. The expression on his face seemed to indicate that any bright side to this situation was escaping him. He looked furious.

"What the hell sort of game are you playing, Josie Pigeon?"

She certainly hadn't expected this sort of response. "I'm not playing any game. I'm doing what I'm supposed to do. I reported finding a dead body, and as you've probably figured out, a murdered body. Because, of course, someone wrapped her in that old cloth and someone must have walled her in . . . I mean, it might have been the same someone, not two someones . . ." She realized she was losing track of the point she had been trying to make. "The woman was murdered. I reported finding her body to the police. To you. So I don't understand why you're angry."

"You don't understand?" Chief Rodney's face was red as a fresh strawberry and getting redder by the minute. "You don't understand?" he repeated. "You think I like people making fun of me?"

"I . . . I wasn't."

"Maybe you'd better come up and take a closer look at your murdered woman."

"I . . ."

"Now!" he roared.

Josie followed him up the stairs. She was shocked by what had happened in the few minutes since she had entered the room. There had been absolutely no attempt made to preserve the crime scene. What was Chief Rodney doing while the rest of the country was watching *CSI* and other crime shows? she wondered, staring at the cloth that was now lying in the middle of the floor. A shoe—no, a leg, she realized—was propped up against a wall.

"She's a dummy," Josie whispered as recognition dawned.

"And you thought I was a dummy and wouldn't realize that fact."

"No, never. I thought she was real. I never imagined anyone would make this up. Why would anyone hide a dummy behind a wall? This makes no sense."

"Oh, it makes sense, Josie Pigeon. You or someone you hired is screwing with the police department—interfering with police business—and that's against the law."

"Is it against the law? Could he arrest me?" A few hours later Josie was stretched out on a well-padded chaise longue set in the middle of the deck behind Sam's house in the dunes. She had a glass of chardonnay produced by a little known Monterey vineyard in one hand, and a cracker piled high with freshly picked crab in the other. Despite the setting and the accoutrements, she was anything but relaxed.

Sam took his time before answering. He took a sip of wine and swished it around in his mouth before swallowing in a manner Josie always found irritating. He held his glass up in the waning light and stared at the pale golden liquid. Josie was considering picking up the plate of crabmeat and using it to hit him over the head when he finally answered her question. "It's possible you might be charged with any number of things, but I can't imagine any of the charges sticking."

"So I don't have to worry, right?"

"I didn't say that. Anytime either of the Rodneys is involved in your life, you should worry. Those two really have it in for you. And I'm beginning to think their new officer is just as bad. She came into the store this afternoon and . . ."

"Sam, I forgot to tell you. She had Tyler in her patrol car last night, in the parking lot at the Wawa."

"Perhaps we should talk about this another time," Sam interrupted. "Here he comes now, and I think that platter he's carrying is filled with Mom's figs and prosciutto."

"Yeah, I am," Tyler said. "You know, this stuff is okay. Sweet and salty at the same time, like a honey pretzel," he said, dropping down and sprawling on a chair (his mother had no idea why he had given up sitting and taken up sprawling on his thirteenth birthday) after leaving the tray precariously resting on the table's edge.

Sam rearranged the tray. "If honey pretzels would make you happy, perhaps you should stick to them. This stuff is almost twenty dollars a pound."

"I really like this," the teen said, and as if to prove it, he stuffed two ham-wrapped fig halves in his mouth at the same time.

"Tyler!"

"Mom, Mrs. Birnbaum said to bring this plate out to you and to help myself," he said after swallowing. "What am I doing wrong?"

Tyler had great grades, perfect SAT scores, and was generally considered intelligent and charming. As he stuffed another fig in his mouth, his mother couldn't imagine why.

Sam grabbed some of the figs before they could vanish. "I gather you and my mother haven't figured out a solution to your problem."

"Nope. I suggested *Carol* since that's what Mom calls her, but Mrs. Birnbaum thinks that's too impersonal. Then I got this really cool idea: *Top Mama*, but I guess she doesn't think it's as cool as I do."

"She might have a point there. I'm sure you two will figure out something eventually."

"Yeah, we're both really smart."

"What are you trying to figure out?" Josie asked.

"What to call Sam's mom. She's going to be my step-grandmother after you and Sam get married, right?"

"Good point," Josie said. She took a deep breath and changed the subject. "You know, I was wondering about last night when I saw you and . . ."

"I gotta go, Mom. I promised Mrs. Birnbaum that I'd help in the kitchen."

As the sliding glass door closed behind Tyler, Sam said, "Well, whatever was going on last night, he's sure not anxious to talk to you about it."

"And that's what worries me. I can't think of a single good reason for him to have been in the police cruiser."

"It's probably something perfectly innocent," Sam said. "Good cops try to get to know the community. I don't think you have anything to worry about."

Josie didn't agree. In fact, she had so many things to worry about that she was beginning to lose count.

EIGHT

Leslie found the second body. He had gone into the crawl space under the house searching for the water main shut-off valve and discovered another blond-wigged manikin stuffed behind a false ceiling near the water meter. When he climbed out, filthy and with silky cobwebs in his hair, and announced his discovery, Josie, Nic, Mary Ann, and Vicki crawled underneath the house without hesitating.

"This is really weird," Leslie said and no one disagreed with him. "I suppose we should get her—it—out of here and call the police."

"There's no need to call anyone," Nic said.

"But we called the police yesterday," Vicki reminded her.

"Only because we thought we had discovered a dead body," Josie said. "The police aren't interested in this junk." She poked the dummy with her finger. "And neither am I. Let's get this thing out of here and get back to work. Leslie, would you toss this in the Dumpster?"

"Yeah, no problem."

Josie led her crew back outside. There was a fresh sea breeze and the sun was shining. She felt like shit. The previous night's dinner had been delicious—and completely unsatisfactory. Sam's mother had found it impossible to hide her enthusiasm for the wedding and had been full of suggestions for the service as well as the reception. She had even brought out the little candles shaped like wedding cakes. Josie, who had not yet made a guest list, was certainly not ready to think about favors. Sam seemed to know how Josie felt, but when he attempted to change the subject by mentioning a cruise his mother had taken a few months before, Carol offered suggestions for possible honeymoon locales. And when Josie brought up the house Island Contracting was working on, Carol had asked whether or not Josie was going to alter Sam's house in any way after they were married.

Tyler was absolutely no help at all. His enthusiastic participation in any conversation about the wedding would have led anyone listening to suspect he was trying to avoid another subject—and that's exactly what Josie did think. Then her son took off, claiming to have a date immediately after dinner. He had arrived back home after Josie was asleep, and he was still in bed when she left that morning.

A completely unsatisfactory evening, and now another stupid manikin.

She was trying not to ask herself what else could go wrong when Christopher Higgins walked around the corner of the house. Josie frowned. His appearance would waste her time if nothing else. He met her frown with a smile. "I come bearing gifts: bagels, lox, and cream cheese," Christopher announced. He held up a large brown bag.

"Cool," Leslie said, pulling the dummy up the last

few steps and dragging it toward the Dumpster that now stood in the middle of the backyard.

"What the hell is that?" Christopher asked.

"What does it look like?" Josie asked.

"To tell you the truth, it looks like a bride," he answered seriously.

"Huh?"

"Yeah. Long blond hair, long white dress . . . I mean, it sort of looks like someone was making a dummy of a bride."

"You know, he's right," Mary Ann said, walking closer to examine the wig and clothing hanging off the dummy. "It does look sort of like a bride—or someone going to a prom or something."

"The one yesterday didn't, though," Vicki pointed out.

"Yesterday?" Christopher asked.

Josie didn't think he had to know anything about that. "We found a bunch of stuff behind one of the walls we knocked down yesterday. It's not that unusual. Workers—not my workers, but some workers—dump debris and garbage behind walls before they're closed in. It's easier than making an extra trip to the Dumpster. But you don't have to worry. No one from Island Contracting would do anything like that."

"I hope not. Food wrappers and that sort of garbage might attract rodents, and we certainly don't want that."

"Of course not," Josie agreed and then asked him a question. "Why are you here?"

"You mean you don't think I'm just playing delivery boy?" he teased.

She didn't have time to fool around, and neither did her crew. "No. Why?" she repeated.

"I wanted to check out a few changes with you . . ."

This was one of the phrases Josie least wanted to hear.

". . . before Luigi arrives to check out the house."

"I'm sorry. I must have missed something. Who is Luigi? One of your relatives?" Josie asked.

"Luigi is my grandmother's decorator. He decorated my grandparent's New York townhouse—more than once, in fact. He also has a client here, a woman who owns one of those big houses up in the dunes. A Mrs. Fairchild. Maybe you know her?"

"No." Josie neglected to add that she usually didn't socialize with the island's elite.

"Grandmother and Mrs. Fairchild are old friends, and when my grandfather heard that Luigi was going to be down here, he asked him to look in on our project. I think they're checking up on me," he added. The smile had vanished from his face.

Josie realized Christopher wasn't any happier with this surprise visit than she was. "How long do you think Luigi will be on the island?"

"I don't know. Maybe just a few days. He has lots of clients in the city—I would assume he has to get back to them sometime soon."

Josie thought it was time to put Christopher out of his misery. "This might just work out for us. I have lots of decisions for your grandmother to make. None of the bathroom fixtures or the tiles for the kitchen backsplash have been selected. Maybe Luigi can look around and then help your grandmother pick out what is appropriate. He'll have a lot to keep himself occupied."

"What about those bagels and lox? I don't know

about the rest of you, but I'm starving," Leslie reminded them all, changing the subject.

Christopher passed around the food, but Josie, though hungry, was not easily distracted. "Do you know if there's anything in particular Luigi has come to see?"

"No. Well, I don't know." Christopher picked up a bagel half and smeared it with cream cheese. "To tell you the truth, Luigi works more closely with Grandmother than Grandfather, and I don't think Grandmother was all that enthusiastic about Grandfather allowing me to remodel this house."

"Really?" Josie resisted smiling. It sounded as though she and Mrs. Higgins had something in common.

"Yeah. I heard her talking to him when they didn't know I was in the room next door, and she said it made no sense." He stopped eating for a moment. "I shouldn't be surprised. Everyone in my class is jealous—no one else will have a senior thesis project like mine. No one else has relatives who will let them do something like this to a house they just bought."

"Perhaps your classmates' families aren't . . . well, don't have the resources your family does," Josie suggested.

The young man brightened up considerably. "You know, you're probably right. It might not have anything at all to do with my professional qualifications." Or lack thereof, Josie thought. "And it might just be that no one else bought a house this year."

She decided it was time to return to the task at hand. "It would be a big help if you could convince your grandmother to pick out appliances and bath fixtures sometime soon. Not that we need to get them in immediately, but if we can place the orders we'll be sure they're here when we need them. Otherwise the end of the project might be delayed, and I know you're interested in finishing on time—right?"

"Yeah, even early would be nice," Christopher enthused. "Then I could take a short break. Maybe spend a few weeks in the Hamptons before school starts."

Josie didn't comment. She wasn't sure which would be worse: having him around and wasting her time for the entire project, or having to push the completion date so he could "spend a few weeks" relaxing before his classes began. "Look, I appreciate being given advance notice of Luigi's arrival and we're all going to enjoy the food you brought, but you did mention some changes you wanted to discuss," she reminded him.

"Oh yeah, well, I was talking to my grandfather last night and I began to worry about storage."

"Closets?"

"Yeah, closets and less conventional storage spaces. This place doesn't have a basement, you know, and so all the stuff that families usually keep in the basement must be kept somewhere."

"One of the garage bays was being used."

"Yeah, but my grandfather specifically mentioned a place to store his fishing gear . . ."

"The garage would be perfect."

". . . in the house," he finished his thought.

Josie frowned. This was one of those ideas that could diminish Island Contracting's profit margin, unless she was careful. "We could increase the size of that small porch behind the kitchen."

"And enclose it, right?" Christopher seemed enthusiastic about that idea. "Then Grandfather could bring his stuff right in from a day at the beach and leave it there.

It would keep the house much cleaner, which Grand-mother would love."

"But it would increase the cost of the project, possibly by as much as fifteen thousand dollars," she finished.

The enthusiasm vanished. "Oh. That might be a problem. You see, Grandfather thinks I . . . I don't want Grandfather to think . . ."

"You forgot he wanted it and now you want it in the plans without him realizing that," Josie guessed.

"Sort of. Do you think we could add the porch and maybe decrease costs someplace else? You know, find some extra money in the project?"

Josie was tempted to tell him that if he ever hired a contracting company that put fifteen thousand dollars' worth of slush in a project, he had hired the wrong company. But Christopher was young. He would learn, and it wasn't her job to teach him. "I think we'll have to talk to your grandfather about increasing the final cost of the project before we touch that porch."

"Well, I'd appreciate it if you didn't mention this to my grandfather. I can handle it, but I'd rather do it in my own way. Okay?"

"Sure."

"Christopher, what are you up to?" came a voice from behind them. "Why, I remember you when you were just a baby and now look at you—designing houses for your grandparents!"

Tight designer jeans, a deep reddish-purple silk shirt, Gucci loafers worn without socks, and hair dyed a brown so dark it was almost magenta. Luigi had arrived.

NINE

T HE HIGGINSES WEREN'T willing to accept second-best, and Luigi was here to see that they didn't get it. He made that point more than once in the hours he spent examining the Bride's Secret Bed and Breakfast. He didn't like anything. Nothing was as Seymour Higgins had described it to him, and Luigi wasn't the least bit reticent when it came to expressing his disappointment.

"This place is horrible. I know that this sort of mid-century crap is popular in some circles, but so inappropriate for a woman of your grandmother's class and sensibilities. I was expecting something very different—very, very different. Something with an air of romance. At the very least some ambience. You do know how this place got its name, don't you?"

"I don't think so," Christopher answered. Josie thought he looked as though he couldn't care less.

"There was a murder here—a murder for love." His emerald-green eyes (contacts, Josie guessed) opened wide, and Luigi told the tale. "This place was built as a wedding present from a man to his future wife. It may not look like much now, but supposedly at that time it was incredible. There weren't many big houses on this island in those days, and this one was the biggest and grandest of them all. People came by train from Philadelphia and New York City just to see it."

"So that's why Grandfather bought this house—to tell my grandmother that he loves her as much as the man who built this place loved his wife."

Luigi made a skeptical sound. "He'd better hope she loves him more than that bride did. This place is called the bride's secret, not the wife's secret."

"I don't get it," Christopher said.

"The story is that they never got married. She vanished the night before the wedding. No one on the island ever saw her again."

"You're kidding."

"No. Your grandfather said there were rumors, of course."

"What sort of rumors?"

"Apparently the architect also vanished. Some people said that he fell in love with the woman while building the house, and they ran off to California the night before the wedding. But apparently there were a lot of people who thought that while the affair might have happened, the trip to California was, alas, wishful thinking. Your grandfather believes that the man who built the house found out about the affair, killed his fiancée, hid her somewhere on the property, and then moved into the house to be near her body. So romantic, don't you think?"

"Not really," Josie answered, but Luigi wasn't interested in her answer.

"Mr. Seymour Higgins and I think the story is very, very romantic. Mr. Higgins said that when he worked here while in college, there were brochures on the hallway table in case guests were interested in the building's history. Although naturally those brochures didn't mention the ghosts."

"What ghosts?" Josie asked.

"As I understand the story, some people claim that the bride's body was concealed in the walls. And that her ghost—and the ghost of her murderer—roam the hallways during storms." He shrugged his silk-clad shoulders. "I never believe that crap, but I cannot believe this is the same Bride's Secret Bed and Breakfast that your grandmother and grandfather described to me."

He wasn't talking about the demolition. Apparently Christopher's grandparents had waxed lyrical about the Bride's Secret, omitting the extensive changes made in the last forty years. Josie, who had followed Luigi downstairs and had noticed the tell-tale tiny scars behind his ears, was tempted to suggest that the house had not benefited from as much nipping and tucking as some people had. But she said nothing, merely taking notes when Luigi actually said something that she could use.

To give Christopher credit, he had made all the right suggestions, even offering a pile of catalogues from which to choose toilets, tiles, refrigerators. Everything was rejected.

Luigi was here to look around, to get a feel for the place. But except for a few impractical suggestions concerning additional closet space, anything that might move the project along was ignored. And he wasn't interested in what they had accomplished. Josie pointed out the work they had done, the demolition, even the places where the dummies had been found. Luigi listened and then changed the subject back to himself and his work. "I simply cannot make decisions in any foreign environment. I need my own space. My office, my city."

"And isn't this incredibly hideous?" They were in the kitchen, and Josie could only agree that there was nothing at all appealing or even practical about the small space. But she couldn't just demolish the room and then leave it empty. Someone had to make some decisions. She was about to explain this when Mary Ann stuck her head around the corner and waved. "Josie, when you have a minute . . ." She vanished.

"I think someone on my crew needs me."

"I believe I need you now," Luigi answered. "I want to get everything in my mind before I see dear Seymour and Tilly."

The Higgins were paying the bills, so Josie had no choice but to listen. "Of course. I'll just close this door. I can't imagine why it's open. She reached out for the knob and realized that Vicki was standing on the top step.

"We need you!" Vicki whispered urgently.

"I'm busy in here," Josie answered loudly. "You know Luigi needs my help right now. I'll come on out when I'm free."

"But . . ."

"Later." Josie slammed the door in her worker's face.

Christopher finally spoke up. "You know, Luigi, there are some beautiful homes on the island. There are some wonderful local workers."

"Isn't she local?" Luigi stared at Josie's jeans, work boots, and unmanicured nails as though he couldn't imagine any other possibility.

"Yes, Josie is a contractor—a carpenter," Christopher said.

Luigi peered at Josie. "I'm sorry. I don't believe I remember your name."

"It's Pigeon. Josie Pigeon."

"What an odd name, I don't believe I've ever met anyone named Pigeon before."

"Josie owns the best contracting company on the island," Christopher said, making Josie feel a bit better.

"I know who she is. I just didn't remember her name there for a moment. It was a very long drive here from the city. The traffic was horrible. I really should have a nice lunch—perhaps a small crab salad and a nice glass of Vouvray—and lie down for a bit. I hate to admit it, but I'm not as young as I used to be, you know."

"Why don't you both go to lunch at Basil's new place?" Josie suggested quickly.

The idea didn't seem to appeal to Luigi. "Is it here on the island? I have a very sensitive stomach and I can eat only very fresh food, prepared in the best continental manner."

"The restaurant has been reviewed favorably in *The New York Times*," Josie said. "It's considered one of the best restaurants in town."

"Really? *The New York Times*?" Luigi said slowly. "Perhaps I have heard about it."

"Basil Tilby owns it. In fact, he owns several restaurants on the island. You may know of him. He's been interviewed on the Food Network more than once, and there was an article written about his fish dishes in *Gourmet* magazine last June," Josie added.

"I think we might just try it for lunch."

Josie realized she wasn't included in this invitation. Not that she cared. "Take your time. I'll be here when you get back," she said to Christopher, hoping he would drop Luigi in the ocean on the way.

"I have many people to see this afternoon. If I don't

come back, you will understand," Luigi said starting for the door.

"If he doesn't come back, I know you'll be thrilled," Christopher whispered to Josie. He grinned, then followed the decorator from the room.

No sooner was he gone than Mary Ann and Vicki appeared.

"Are they gone for a while?" Vicki asked.

"Are they going to be back soon?" Mary Ann asked.

"They went to lunch. I hope we never see Luigi again. I can't imagine what the Higginses were thinking when they suggested he come down here and waste our time. But that's not our problem. We need to get back to work. Where's Leslie?" Josie asked.

"He's with the body. We didn't want to leave it alone," Mary Ann explained.

"That stupid thing!" Josie exploded. "Put it in the Dumpster and let's get on with this job."

"You don't understand," Vicki said.

"No, we found another body. A real one," Mary Ann explained.

"Damn. I guess we're going to have to call the police," Josie said.

TEN

JOSIE WAS EXPECTING Mike Rodney or his father to respond to her call, and she didn't know whether to be pleased or concerned when Trish Petric stepped out of the police cruiser. Josie knew the Rodneys would cause problems, but she found herself longing for the devil she knew.

"We got some sort of stupid prank call about another body," Trish said immediately.

"I called . . ." Josie began.

"It's illegal to waste police time," Trish interrupted.

"I don't think you're going to find this a waste of your time. There's a dead woman on the floor in the master bedroom suite," Josie explained.

"Yeah, right. Of course. So why are you all sitting out here on the porch if there's a body inside?"

Nic looked around at her fellow workers. "I guess no one wanted to stay in there with her. I know I sure didn't. She gives me the creeps."

Trish looked disgusted. "Perhaps the person who shows me the body should be someone who doesn't get the creeps so easily."

Josie had been leaning against a post supporting the roof of the porch, and she shifted her weight to her feet.

"I'll go in with you. Leslie, Vicki, Mary Ann, and Nic can wait out here for the rest of your department."

"I'm alone on this one," Trish informed them. "The Chief and his son are busy."

"You're kidding. There's a dead body in the house. What are they doing that could be more important than being here?" Nic asked.

For the first time Trish looked a bit less confident. "They're down on the dock making sure the state's non-resident saltwater fishing regulations are posted."

"It takes two grown men to do that?" Leslie asked.

"They're fishing. Or crabbing," Josie explained. "And if the blues are running early this year, they may decide to check out some of the charter boats that go out as well."

"Making sure state fishing regulations are enforced is an important duty of police departments in shore areas," Trish insisted.

"Yeah, right." Josie knew those "duties" would be quickly forgotten when the Rodneys heard about her crew's latest discovery. "So do you want to see the body now?"

"I'm not the one slowing us down asking questions."

Josie opened the door and entered the house. She didn't bother to reply to Trish's criticism.

Leslie and Vicki had discovered the body as they began pulling the wooden panels off the walls upstairs. According to Vicki, the body, tightly wrapped in a blanket, had been dumped in a space left when the wall was wrapped around the chimney leading from the living room fireplace to the roof. Josie explained this as she led the police officer up the stairs. "When the walls were paneled, I guess someone figured leaving an unusually large space would protect the paneling from any heat escaping from the chimney. Not that it would. It really wasn't safe at all, and certainly not up to code," she added, opening the door and standing back so Trish could precede her into the room.

"Oh my God. She's real," declared Officer Petric.

Leslie had unwound the royal blue Hudson Bay blanket which had surrounded the body and revealed maroon dried bloodstains on the woman's back.

The police officer walked a few steps into the room and then stopped, fumbling for the cell phone hanging from her belt. "I need to call in about this. I need . . . uh, I think I need backup."

Josie knew she had the unfortunate distinction of having viewed more murder victims than most people, but she was still surprised by the police officer's obvious discomfort. Trish was, after all, a professional, and it wasn't as though the scene before them was particularly gory. The body lay on the floor, face toward the wall. Except for the bloodstains and the location, the woman might have been taking a nap. Her long blond hair straggled down her back and mixed with the dried blood covering her pressed dark cotton shirt. A long white shirt and deck shoes worn without socks completed her outfit. No one, as far as Josie knew, had turned the body over to examine her more carefully. Apparently Trish wasn't going to do it, either. She had moved over into a corner as far away as it was possible to get without leaving the room to make her phone call. Josie leaned against the doorjamb and waited for the arrival of the rest of the island's police force. She heard her crew moving around downstairs, chatting together quietly. "I should go and . . ."

Trish looked up. "I'd prefer you to stay right where you are."

"Oh, okay. It's just that I hate wasting time and my crew could be working in another part of the house."

"I said I'd prefer you to stay right where you are," Trish repeated.

Josie realized there was nothing to be gained by arguing. Besides, she was amused by the police woman's avoidance of the body. Trish was circling the dead woman, examining her without moving in for a closer look, frowning with one hand on the butt of her gun as though she expected some sudden movement on the part of the cadaver. Downstairs, the squeal of old wood splitting signaled a renewal of demolition. Josie just hoped no more bodies were discovered. She looked up, realizing Trish was speaking to her and not into her phone. "Excuse me?"

"I asked you if you knew her . . . if you could ID the dead woman."

Josie wondered if Trish watched the same cop shows she did. "No. I guess she couldn't be the missing bride, though. Too recently killed."

"What do you know about a missing bride?"

Josie was surprised by the sharpness of the question. Apparently Trish was even more upset by this discovery than she had imagined. "It's the legend of the house, before it was a bed-and-breakfast," she said, and then repeated the story Luigi had told just a few hours before.

Trish wasn't impressed. "Of course she couldn't be the bride. That's one of the stupidest things I've ever heard. In the first place, all anyone has to do is look around to realize that this place has been remodeled more than once. If the so-called bride's body had been concealed here, someone would have found her before now. And, besides, you're talking about something that was supposed to have happened decades ago, right?"

"Yes, the house was built back in the early forties, sometime before World War Two."

"And does that woman look like someone who has been dead since then?"

"No, of course not. That's exactly what I was saying. It's just that there's this legend and now this body . . . I wasn't thinking. It's so odd. There are so many coincidences."

"What do you mean?"

"Well, look at her. She looks like those dummies. It's like someone wanted us to find her after finding the dummies."

"Dummies? I understood there was one dummy found here."

"We found another, but we didn't want to bother the police with it."

Trish frowned.

"The point I was making is that it's odd to find the dummies and then to find her. It doesn't make sense, does it?" Josie stopped speaking.

"Not to me. But you probably know more about this than I do."

"What do you mean?"

"Well, someone on your crew found these dummies you're talking about, and then found her, right?"

"Right."

"And maybe that person knew what order to find them in."

"That's not possible. They were all working together when the woman was found."

The sound of screen doors slamming against the walls in the foyer announced the arrival of the rest of the island's police force. "Paaaattty, where the hell are you?"

Josie recognized the voice as belonging to Chief Rodney, unhappy to have his fishing interrupted. She wondered why he was the only person who didn't call his new deputy Trish. Perhaps they had a personal relationship?

"Up here, Chief. In the master bedroom with the body. And Josie Pigeon," she added.

Josie wasn't thrilled to be included almost as an afterthought. "I wanted to go back downstairs and work with my crew," she said as Chief Rodney and his son appeared in the doorway. "We do have a job to do here, you know. Officer Petric didn't want me to leave this room for some reason."

"Did you find her?" Chief Rodney had gained more than a little weight in the past few years and he squatted awkwardly over the body, tilting back and forth as he tried to balance. After a few seconds, he snorted and stood up with much creaking of knees, ankles, and hips.

"No, my workers did."

"I'll wanna talk to those ladies as soon as possible."

"Those ladies?" Josie recognized his assumption. "Not only ladies, Chief. Leslie found her. He's a man."

"Not a member of the fairer sex? That's quite a departure for Island Contracting, isn't it, Miss Pigeon?"

"We've had men on the crew before," she stated.

"Yeah, well, I know there are some people who think you should do that a little more often. Someone was making a joke about Island Contracting's coven just the other day."

"Who? Where?"

"Sure don't want to be telling tales out of school, but it just might have been someone down at the Fish Wish Bait Shop. Perhaps you know someone down there who might feel a little resentful when he thinks about your company and its chauvinistic hiring practices?"

Before Josie could protest that Leslie's presence on the job proved Island Contracting didn't have any chauvinistic hiring practices, Mike Rodney Junior, leaning over the body, spoke up.

"Of course, maybe they weren't talking about the sex of your workers—maybe they were thinking about all the dead bodies that seem to appear when you and your ladies are around."

Josie was too angry to think of an appropriately scathing response.

ELEVEN

"THIS HAS BEEN one of the worst days of my life."

Risa, Josie's landlady, placed a large platter of antipasto on the table before her. "You just sit back and taste this tuna focaccia. I make the bread with flour from chicken peas—flour not easy to find in this country. Good food will help you relax. Good food very important. Good food make a party."

Josie speared a shrimp that had been grilled with fresh herbs, put it in her mouth, and chewed thoughtfully before asking a question. "Chicken peas? What are chicken peas?"

"Little round things, you find them on those awful salad bars. You know them."

Enlightenment dawned. "I think you mean chick-peas."

"Chicken peas. Chickpeas. Makes no difference what you call them. Difference is in using them to make flour—flour from wheat will not make these as good. And good food important for parties."

Josie looked up from the delicious display. "Who is giving a party?"

"You! You and Sam will give party when you are married!"

"We . . ." Light dawned. "You mean our wedding reception!"

Risa nodded vigorously, her long dark hair flying about, the layers of silk that made up her clothing rippling. "Yes. Wedding reception that someone must cook for."

"I don't know if there's going to be a wedding."

"What?" It was almost a shriek. "No wedding? How can that be? The whole island look forward to your wedding. Everyone talk about it. You and Sam just have nervous nerves. You be fine. You will have wedding."

"The whole island?" Josie repeated Risa's words, momentarily distracted from the problem at hand.

"The whole island. You and Sam may fight, but you and Sam make up. Everyone waiting for your wedding. I shall go to New York City to buy beautiful new dress and pair of those pointy tall shoes that women on TV wear."

"That's more than I've done," Josie admitted. "But, Risa, Sam and I aren't fighting. It's just that I've found a body in the house I'm working on."

"Ah, you find the bride at the Bride's Secret Bed and Breakfast?"

"You've heard that story?" Josie was surprised.

"Yes, of course. I once thought to maybe buy that house. The realtor who showed house to me told me about ghost. Not that I believe in dead people coming back. But I believe in murder, of course. Now. Now because I know you."

Josie understood that Risa was referring to her own experience with dead bodies, not making an oblique threat. But she had another question. "When did you think about buying that place?"

"Long time ago. Before you move to island and bring Tyler into world. I want to make more money renting more places, and Bride's Secret Bed and Breakfast was place where that could have happen—not that last owners do, but I could have done. But then you and Tyler move in here and . . ." She shrugged her elegant shoulders, sending a long turquoise scarf scudding to the floor. "And once you and Tyler here, I know nothing else need to happen."

Josie sat for a moment, taking it all in. Risa would have made more money—a lot more money—renting out apartments in that big building rather than making do with the small rent she charged Josie, to say nothing of the hours and hours of free babysitting Risa had provided, along with what must quite literally be thousands of delicious free meals. And now Risa wanted to take part in her wedding—was asking to work, for heaven's sake. Josie realized she had no choice but to gratefully accept her offer. And that's what she was doing when Mike Rodney drove up.

Josie and Risa had been seated at a white metal table on Risa's screened-in porch. The summer before, Hurricane Agatha had badly damaged this side of the house, and Josie had rebuilt and expanded the porch over the winter. Watching Mike stamp up the sidewalk to the house, she only wished she had replaced the screens with a solid wall. She did not want to talk to him, but unfortunately, he had a clear view of her through the new screens.

"Josie. We need to talk to you immediately," he announced halfway to the steps.

"We?" Risa asked. "I do not see a we. I see a me. Only a me."

Mike was on the top step waiting for someone to open the door and he frowned at her words. "It's a figure of speech. American speech," he added, rather nastily.

Josie jumped to Risa's defense. "Risa is an American. She became a citizen a few years ago."

"Funny, she don't talk like one."

Josie was about to protest his statement, if not his grammar, when Risa spoke up for herself. "I take test to become American citizen. I learn about United States of American Constitution. I know you cannot enter my house unless I allow you to do so."

Mike's hand had been on the door knob and he froze, glaring at the two women through the screen door.

"I think we should ask him in," Josie suggested, hoping no one could detect from her voice how much she was enjoying this encounter.

"Or I could have someone come and arrest you both for obstructing a legitimate police investigation into the murder of an unknown man."

"Woman," Josie interrupted.

"I think you cannot do that," Risa spoke up, still trying to show what she had learned for her citizen's exam. "I think . . ."

"I think you can let me come in now or I will get a warrant and bring Miss Josie Pigeon down to the station for questioning. And I mean it!" Mike's voice was approaching a roar.

"I think we should invite him in," Josie said again. "I'd rather talk to him here than at the police station."

Risa quickly changed her tactics. "And you both sit and have some of my antipasto while you talk. I get another plate and fork." She swept off to the kitchen as the policeman, not waiting for an invitation, slumped into the seat she had vacated.

"You found another body," Josie guessed.

"Lord, no. What's wrong with you? Isn't one body per remodeling job enough?"

"You mentioned a dead man."

"The guy you found at the Bride's Secret Bed and Breakfast this morning."

"In the first place, I didn't find him. One of my crew found him. In the second place, he found a woman, not a man."

"A man disguised as a woman."

Josie blinked. "Huh?"

"Not much of a disguise, either," the officer added, helping himself to the largest bruschetta and popping it in his mouth. "Just that damn wig plopped on his head. You wouldn't think it would fool anyone for long," he added, chewing.

"I don't understand. Are you telling me that the body we found—the one wrapped in a Hudson Bay blanket—was a man? And that he was wearing a blond wig to look like a woman?"

"Yeah, that's just what I'm saying. Anything complicated about that?"

"Not really." Josie answered slowly. "Do you know who the man is? Did anyone recognize him?"

A small pile of shrimp disappeared into Mike Rodney's mouth before he answered. "Nope. Course no one's looked at him either, except Dad and me and our cute new department employee. Made her a bit sick to tell the truth. She's been sort of pale and quiet ever since."

"Is that why you're here? Do you want me to see if I recognize him?"

"Why? Do you think you know him?"

"I have no idea. How would I know if I know . . ." Josie decided to give up. "Exactly why are you here?" she asked.

Mike leaned forward and pulled a roll of papers from his back pocket. "Got some questions about your crew."

"What sort of questions? Officer Petric took statements from everyone just a few hours ago."

"Yeah, but we ran their names through the computer down at the station and came up with some interesting facts." He swiped the last shrimp off the plate and stuffed it in his mouth.

Josie hoped he would choke on it. "What facts?" she asked.

"Let's see . . . they're all right here." He slowly unrolled the sheets and appeared to reread them. Josie suspected he was doing it merely to irritate her. Perhaps she could convince Risa to add one of those undetectable poisons that mystery novelists were so fond of to her next batch of scampi.

"You hired some real interesting women this time, Miss Pigeon . . ."

"Yes, I did. They're competent workers as well as strong people." She picked up a round of tender fried squid and ate it. Delicious. Absolutely delicious.

"This Leslie guy is a terror on the highway—he had so many tickets that he had to go to court to prove he couldn't earn a living without having a license the last time it came up for renewal."

"That's why you're here? What else? Does Mary Ann have a pile of unpaid parking violations? Perhaps Vicki was once ticketed for jaywalking? Maybe Nic . . ." she ran out of ideas.

Unfortunately, Mike Rodney hadn't. "Maybe Nic was once arrested for murder," he said, smiling and chewing and talking at the same time.

Josie gasped at his words although his appearance was pretty appalling as well. "What are you saying? What do you mean, 'maybe?' Was she or wasn't she?"

"She was."

"Being arrested isn't the same thing as being convicted," Josie pointed out.

"Yeah, but just because a case is hard to prove doesn't mean it ain't legit. Ask any cop. Besides," he swallowed and grinned, "she was convicted. Even spent time in prison."

Josie didn't know what to say. Fortunately, Risa had returned. As promised, she had a plate, silverware, and napkin in hand. And she was followed by Sam Richardson.

"Sam! What are you doing here?" The question was out of Josie's mouth before she realized that Risa must have called him from the phone in the kitchen.

Sam smiled, walked over to her chair, kissed the top of Josie's head, and placed a protecting hand on her shoulder before answering. "I always think it's interesting to appear anyplace where a police cruiser is parked. You never know what you'll discover."

"You heard about the dead man down on Josie's work site, right?" Rodney asked.

"The fact is, Josie didn't see fit to share that information with me," Sam answered. Josie felt his fingers tighten on her shoulder, but his voice betrayed nothing.

"Yeah, the guy was stabbed to death before someone

popped a blond wig on his head, wrapped him in a blanket, and stuffed him behind a wall just waiting for one of Josie's crew to find him. Course, who woulda known that one of the people to find him was convicted of murder just awhile ago herself?"

No one had any idea what to say about that. The only sound in the room was chewing as Mike Rodney scarfed up Risa's fine food.

TWELVE

THE NEXT MORNING when none of her employees showed up for work, Josie knew her company was facing its most serious crisis since she inherited it. Alone in her office, she was wondering what to do when her son appeared in the doorway. Nothing else could have cheered her up. She was so pleased to see him that she didn't ask about the large cardboard box he carried in his arms. Besides, she didn't have to ask: plaintive mewing preceded a tiny white head peeping out of a hole in the cardboard.

"I hope you have enough kitten chow for this gang," Tyler said, placing the box on the floor with more care than he usually displayed.

Josie tried hard not to sigh or make any gesture that could indicate disapproval. "How many? And where did they come from?"

"Six. They were found next to the Dumpster by the Dairy Queen. Two are pure white—they're amazing. Wait until you see." Tyler had opened the box and he slowly tipped it on its side, allowing the kittens to venture into their new environment in their own time. A caramel-colored tiger flew out and raced around the room. His brothers and sisters followed more cautiously.

"Have you had breakfast yet?" Josie asked.

"Just a bowl of cereal and some . . . some juice."

Josie suspected her son's "juice" had come out of a Coke can, but she didn't say anything. "Want to come to Sullivan's with me? We could have pancakes and sausage if you're still hungry." She knew he was always hungry.

"Yeah, but don't you have to get to work?"

"I can be a little late today. After all, I'm the boss." Josie smiled at her son and hoped he wasn't remembering all the times she had explained that being the boss meant setting an example—starting work early, leaving late.

"Yeah. There weren't a lot of you when Noel died, were there, Mom?"

She wasn't sure exactly what he was asking. "Women who owned contracting companies, or female carpenters?"

"Both, I guess."

Josie glanced up at her handsome son while searching in her jeans pockets for the keys to her truck. She had been a working mother all his life; she couldn't remember him ever asking questions about her work, and was deeply pleased by his interest. "Well, things have changed a bit since I started working for Noel . . ." she began, opening the door for them both.

By the time they had traveled the five or six miles between her office and Sullivan's General Store, she had pretty much reviewed her early years with Island Contracting and had begun to explain how bookkeeping and paperwork had entered her life after Noel's death. She found a parking spot directly outside the store and followed Tyler in the door.

Sullivan's was a local institution. At one time the only store on the north end of the island, it had moved twenty years ago to its Ocean Drive location and expanded to include a small kitchen, a long lunch counter, and some small Formica-topped tables. Tourists loved the place—they rented bicycles and sea kayaks there, bought plastic beach toys and boogie boards for their children when it was sunny, and purchased playing cards, games, and jigsaw puzzles when it rained. Josie usually came for the food. The eggs were prepared on griddles that had been producing crisp bacon and well-done sausage patties for two decades, and the result was delicious. She asked for the usual when she sat down, and knew two fried eggs, their edges crispy, their yokes slightly runny, would appear surrounded by strips of bacon, fresh hash browns, and a pile of buttered rye toast. Tyler was more unpredictable: he always had a difficult time choosing between pancakes and French toast. This morning, he wanted pancakes and sausages. He didn't sit down until he had personally spoken to the chef and both waitresses, and his mother knew he would find double orders of everything on the plate when his meal arrived.

Naturally, everyone in the place was talking about the body, and it wasn't long before the questions—and teasing—began.

"There's a rumor going around that your mother's company has got another body on its hands," their waitress, a girl Tyler had grown up with, teased, setting down two glasses of orange juice on their table.

"The body has nothing to do with Island Contracting," Josie protested.

"Chief Rodney was in earlier, and that's not what he

'said," she explained. "He said the body was someone on your crew."

"He what? That's not right. You must have misunderstood. Someone on my crew discovered the body, that's all."

The young woman frowned, but she didn't argue. "I must have misunderstood. I heard that it was someone on your crew. But then it was a man, wasn't it? And everyone knows you don't hire men."

"That's not exactly true." Josie would have explained further, but their food arrived, steaming and fragrant.

Tyler was tall and thin, but he enjoyed a high-calorie, high-fat meal as much as his mother. They didn't speak again until the bottoms of their plates could be seen. "Risa says she's going to cook for your wedding reception," Tyler commented, pouring about a quarter cup of maple syrup on the last and previously saturated pancake on his plate.

"She's been so wonderful to us, I really couldn't refuse."

"But where are you going to hold it? Our place is too small and anyway, I thought Sam told me that the reception was going to be at one of Basil's restaurants."

Josie looked up from her food. "That's right. Oh sh— oh da—" She gave up trying not to curse in front of her son. "What the hell am I going to do?"

He smiled happily. "I don't know, but you'll figure it out. You know, I have some questions . . ."

But Josie was sitting where she could see through the large windows that looked out onto Ocean Drive and she had an unobstructed view of an Island Contracting truck traveling south. She stood up. "That's my truck. I have to get to work. Tell someone to put our meal on my account. Do you have any cash? Can you leave a tip?"

"Sure. But I'm still hungry. Do you think I could have a bagel and some cream cheese?"

"Anything you want," his mother answered, heading for the door. Tyler knew most of the year-round population on the island and had probably met about half of the summer people in the weeks since he had been home from school. He wouldn't have any trouble getting to where he was going on his own. It was a sign of how confused she was that she didn't stop to wonder exactly where he needed to be that morning; she had to find out who was in that truck and where *they* were going.

She caught up with her truck, and her crew, at the Bride's Secret Bed and Breakfast. Everyone was there except Leslie, and everyone there was huddled around Vicki, who was crying. Josie asked the obvious questions. "What's wrong? Where's Leslie?"

Nic looked up. "Leslie's what's wrong. He's been down at the police station all night."

Vicki stopped crying long enough to speak. "He's been arrested and no one will tell us why!"

Vicki began sobbing even harder. Josie looked around. They were all on the front porch, and although it was still morning, the early beach crowd was passing by, beach chairs slung over their shoulders, towels, books, sunscreen, and all the day's necessities stuffed into brightly colored straw and canvas bags. She and her crew hardly fit in with this cheerful scene. "Let's go inside."

"We can't get in. We don't have a key," Nic pointed out.

Josie pulled the key from her pocket and tossed it to

Nic. "You unlock. I need to make a phone call before I come inside. And you might make some coffee."

"No problem."

Josie ran back to her truck as her crew entered the house. She had her cell phone, but she wanted a bit of privacy to make her call. By the time she joined her crew in the kitchen, the scent of fresh coffee had joined the musty odor of a building in which old walls were coming down. Vicki was holding a steaming mug and sniffling. Josie accepted a mug from Mary Ann and jumped up to sit on the counter. "What exactly is going on?"

"Last night . . . the police . . . Leslie . . ." Vicki seemed unable to complete a sentence.

"Nic can explain. She was there," Mary Ann suggested.

Nic nodded and put down her coffee. "I was over at Vicki and Leslie's apartment last night. We'd rented a bunch of videos and picked up a couple of pizzas. We planned on a nice quiet evening—it had been a long day."

"Then the police . . ." Vicki didn't have to finish her sentence for everyone to know what had happened.

"Did they tell you why they were arresting Leslie?" Josie asked.

"They didn't arrest him. At least not then," Nic said. "They said they wanted him to come down to the police station and answer some questions. Leslie said sure."

"They arrested him!" Vicki wailed.

"You don't know that," Mary Ann said. "They may have just wanted to ask him some questions like they said."

"All night?" Vicki stopped sobbing long enough to interrupt.

"A lot of questions," Mary Ann said.

"So he hasn't come back to the apartment?" Josie asked.

"Noooo!" It was a wail.

Josie asked another question. "Did he call or anything?"

"No one's heard a word," Nic answered.

"Not that that means anything," Mary Ann said.

Josie thought about what she had just heard. "I called Sam as soon as you told me about Leslie, and he's on his way to the station. He'll be able to find out what's going on, unless Leslie doesn't want him to."

"Why Sam?" Mary Ann asked.

"Sam's a lawyer."

"I thought he owned that fancy liquor store a few blocks from here," Nic said.

"He does. He doesn't practice anymore. He used to work in New York City, and he retired and bought the store. But he still has his license."

Vicki stopped crying. "Will he get Leslie out of jail?"

"We don't know that he is in jail," Mary Ann reminded her.

"And Sam won't represent Leslie—although he can help us find someone if Leslie does need a lawyer—but the island police won't dare do anything they shouldn't with Sam around. If Leslie is being held down at the station, well, Sam will make sure everything's okay."

"Sounds like a good thing. The cops on this island are something else."

"That's one way of putting it," Josie said. "But, remember, Sam can't do anything at all unless Leslie allows him to."

Vicki was listening and her tears had stopped flowing. "Do you think Sam can convince Leslie to accept help?"

"I have no idea," Josie said.

"Listen, there's no reason to cry," Nic spoke up. "Leslie's probably just fine. Besides, there are worse things than being arrested for murder."

"How do you know?" Vicki wailed.

"I do know. You see . . ." She took a deep breath. "You see, I was arrested for murder years ago."

"You were arrested for murder?" Josie repeated. So Mike Rodney had been telling the truth.

"Yeah. And convicted," she added, looking down at the floor. "But it was different then. I was different then. It happened when I was in high school and hanging around with the wrong kids. Well, the truth is that I was hung up on the wrong guy."

"Something that's happened to all of us," Mary Ann spoke up.

"But this wrong guy was really wrong—he was involved in a lot of criminal activities and he wanted me to prove how much I loved him by . . . by helping out."

"What did you do?" Mary Ann's eyebrows had risen so high they were hidden by her bangs.

"I was the driver for a convenience store robbery. He said having someone sitting in the car would make the getaway easier. He didn't say he was going to kill the clerk—who was just a kid himself—in his stupid attempt to get enough money for some dime bags." She looked around at her companions. "We were caught, and I was convicted along with him. I spent four years in prison. In fact, that's where I learned my trade. Getting a job was a condition of my parole. A great social worker connected me with a group that puts women in nontraditional jobs. I've been doing this ever since."

"And none of your employers have known about your background?" Josie asked.

"Up until now, they all have. I hoped . . . to tell you the truth, I thought it was time to leave my past behind. You don't ask about a criminal record on Island Contracting's application form, so I figured . . ." Nic shrugged. "I figured that the past was the past and that was it."

"Sounds good to me." The voice came from the doorway where Leslie and Sam were now standing.

"You're not under arrest!" Vicki's face lit up.

"No, the cops don't know what to do with me."

"Why should they do anything with you? You found the body, but what other connection is there?" Josie asked.

"The dead man had my ID in his wallet."

"Your ID?"

"My driver's license," Leslie explained.

"How the hell did that happen?" Nic asked.

"Damned if I know, but it seems to have made me the primary suspect in the guy's murder," Leslie said.

Vicki started to cry again.

THIRTEEN

THEY WERE ALL professionals, and that day they proved it. Despite everything that had happened in the previous twenty-four hours, everyone worked and worked hard. By evening, all that remained on the first floor were support beams, the load-bearing walls, and some of the original woodwork. The room where the body (as yet unidentified) had been found was off limits, but at this rate demolition would be done by the end of the week. Josie needed to check the status of orders at the local hardware store. If everything was in place on the island—and having worked with the same suppliers for over a decade, she expected that to be true—construction would begin the next Monday. She reminded her crew to get to bed early that night and to be on site early the next day—and reminded Leslie and Vicki to call Sam if the police appeared. Then she headed straight for the hardware store.

Island Hardware was an institution. So far it had managed to fend off competition from the massive chain store that was located less than a mile from the north bridge, attracting customers with its huge selection and discount prices. Josie had sworn to herself that Island

Contracting would continue to support local businesses, although she knew her profit margin suffered as a result. On the other hand, she always got extra attention at the store. That night the attention included a mug of coffee and the best coconut cupcakes she had ever tasted.

"My niece is visiting for the summer and she likes to bake," Steve Bradley, the store's owner, explained as he passed Josie another cake.

"She's good—these are wonderful."

"That's what your son seemed to think. I believe he ate an even dozen this afternoon."

"Tyler was here?"

"Yup. Kathy—that's my niece—and he are going out for pizza tonight. She just got back from a trip up to Boston with her parents to check out possible colleges, and they say they're going to be exchanging information. I think your son has a crush on her—which is fine with the wife and me. We've always said Tyler's one of the nicest young men on the island."

"He's never disappointed me," Josie said. She didn't add that he frequently surprised her. She never knew what he was going to do or where he was going to turn up. On the other hand, the same could be said of Mike Rodney. Not all surprises are good ones, she thought as the police officer marched down the store's aisle.

"Josie Pigeon, I need to talk to you," he announced so loudly that everyone in the store could hear.

"I'm not running away from you," she pointed out.

"I need to talk to you down at the station."

"Mike, I'm busy. I have a large home to remodel and . . ."

"You're gonna be remodeling that building from a jail cell unless you come with me."

Josie was startled by his vehemence. "I have to check the status of my order here," she explained, trying to be reasonable. "It won't take more than fifteen minutes."

"I'll give you ten. And I'll be waiting for you in my car out front. I'm parked right next to your truck, so don't think you can sneak off."

Josie didn't bother to ask why she would do that. She turned her back on Mike and returned to her examination of Island Contracting's orders. She heard footsteps and the door swing shut as he left the store. "He's gone," Steve Bradley told her.

"Thank God. I don't know why I let him get to me like that. I don't mind answering questions . . . most of the time," she added. "I don't even know what he needs to ask me about."

"The dead man. Or maybe the fact that the dead man was dressed up as the ghost or the bride or whatever spirit is supposed to haunt the Bride's Secret Bed and Breakfast. The fact that he was carrying the identification papers of one of your new crew members."

Josie, not surprised by the island's strong grapevine, sighed. "Yeah. All that. I guess I may as well forget getting a good night's sleep."

"Look, we'll double-check your order and leave a message at your office if we find a problem. You get over to the police station."

Josie grinned. This was the best reason she could think of to deal with independent local stores. "That would be great. The sooner I get over there, the sooner I'll get home—I hope. Thanks."

"No problem," he answered as the door of his store closed behind her.

Mike Rodney was leaning against his cruiser, smoking a cigarette.

"I thought you quit," Josie commented, heading toward her truck.

"Scientists have discovered that an addiction to nicotine is just as strong as an addiction to heroin," he announced, tossing the butt on the ground and stomping on it.

Josie decided this was no time to bring up the island's anti-littering campaign. "Do you trust me to get to the station on my own or do I have to come in your car?"

She hadn't expected him to take her question seriously, but he actually considered for a moment. "You can take your truck and I'll follow you. No way you can escape that way—your old thing can't outrun me."

Josie, who hadn't even considered escaping, wondered if she should have called Sam before leaving the hardware store. "I'll be sure to stay under the speed limit" was her only statement—said a bit sarcastically—before climbing up into her truck and starting off down the street. Mike Rodney, as promised, followed close behind, lights on the police cruiser pulsing. Despite not looking in her rearview mirror, Josie felt a headache coming on.

Mike's father and Officer Petric were in the lobby, hanging around the dispatcher's desk, seemingly waiting for Josie and her escort to appear.

"I found her," Mike announced loudly.

Josie glanced over at him wondering exactly what was going on. "I wasn't hiding," she explained.

"No place to hide on an island," Chief Rodney explained to his new officer.

"Do you think we could get on with all this?" Josie asked impatiently. "I have a business to run, a child to raise, and . . . a wedding to plan."

"Yeah. Well, we won't keep you longer than absolutely necessary," the chief said. "We need some information about your workers. We coulda gotten a search warrant and just gone into your office files, you know."

Josie, aware of what sort of order her files were in, knew they were unlikely to learn much there. "Are we going to talk here?" she asked after greeting the summer dispatcher. The lobby was the busiest spot in the police station. When the dispatcher wasn't answering calls from residents worried that the smoke billowing from a neighbor's Weber grill was the sign of a house fire, she directed visitors to the booth where beach passes were sold, distributed tide tables, explained fishing regulations, and accepted checks for the numerous speeding tickets the Rodneys issued to drivers going five miles an hour over the island speed limit. The revenues from the latter more than paid her salary.

"We'll go into my office," the Chief announced as though Josie had suggested something else.

Josie was surprised to discover that everyone except for the dispatcher was included. The three officers crowded into Chief Rodney's office. Josie was familiar with the room. Island Contracting had built it after Hurricane Agatha destroyed the municipal center the summer before. Instead of the fake wood paneling that covered the cinder-block walls in the rest of the building, this room had cherry walls and built-in bookshelves wide enough to hold the large flat-screen television the Chief claimed to find essential to his work. Josie noticed a second television monitor, now turned off, and won-

dered if the department was paying large cable bills.
One wall was lined with oak filing cabinets. Three chairs
sat in front of the big oak partners' desk placed in the
middle of the room. The only other furniture was the expensive ergonomically designed desk chair in which the
Chief sat. He pointed to the chair directly in front of
him, which Josie interpreted as an order. Becoming more
and more anxious to get this over with, she sat. The two
officers sat on either side, Trish Petric pulling a notebook from her back pocket and flipping it open, apparently prepared to take notes.

"You act as a secretary as well as a police officer?"
Josie asked.

"She does what I ask her to do," Chief Rodney growled,
but Trish glanced over at her, and Josie thought she saw
a smile flash across the woman officer's face.

"Oh."

"Suppose you pay attention to your situation and forget about women's lib and solidarity and such shit,"
Mike Rodney suggested.

"I don't know what my situation is," Josie pointed
out.

"You are here to help the police investigate the murder of an unknown man," Mike explained.

"You told me I was here to answer questions about
my crew," she reminded him.

"There's no difference between the two things. To our
way of thinking someone on your crew probably killed
the guy, stuffed him behind the wall, then found him,
pretending to be all innocent." Chief Rodney was glaring at Josie in a way that made her appreciate the wide
table between them.

"Why?" she asked quietly.

"Why what?" he growled back.

"Why would anyone on my crew kill someone then stuff them in the wall and then pretend to find them? Why not just kill them and dump them in a Dumpster, or in the ocean, or in a house a different company is remodeling? You would never connect the murder with anyone working for Island Contracting if the body had been found somewhere else." She realized the flaw in her thinking as soon as the words were out of her mouth.

"But the body was found with the driver's license of a man named Leslie Coyne. The same Leslie Coyne who is working for you. So there's that connection," Trish pointed out quietly.

"Yeah, I'd forgotten about that for a sec," Josie admitted.

"You had, had you?" Mike leaned down at her.

"Yes, I had! It's been a difficult few days, and I have a lot on my mind," she ended weakly.

"Yeah. Well, we do, too," Chief Rodney said. "And we're busy here, so why don't you tell us how you came to hire the people on your crew."

"Well, I didn't actually hire them. Not this time," Josie admitted.

"Not this time?" Trish looked up from her note-taking to ask the question.

"No, I usually do, of course. Sometimes I put ads in the trade papers, but mostly I just run a local ad. And people come to me, of course. Island Contracting is well known. I've never had trouble finding workers."

"Yeah, yeah. So everyone wants to work for you. So why didn't you hire the people working for you this summer?" Mike Rodney asked.

"Because Nic did . . . I hired Nic though," Josie pointed out.

Trish was frowning. "You allowed someone else to hire your summer crew?" she asked.

"Sort of."

Trish asked a follow-up question. "Is that usual for Island Contracting?"

"Definitely not," Josie answered.

"Then why . . . ?"

Josie didn't allow her to ask another question. It was time for this to end. The Rodneys were grinning at her obvious discomfort. "Island Contracting is not like other companies," she began, ignoring something that sounded like "no shit" from one of the men. "I try to hire people who need a second chance in life. Nic belongs to an organization of women who work in my business— contractors, owners, carpenters, electricians, everything. And they held a convention in Washington DC a few weeks ago. She met Leslie, Mary Ann, and Vicki there, and offered them jobs with Island Contracting. I knew about it and had given her permission to do so, as long as the people she offered jobs to understood that I have the last word."

"Why don't you belong to this organization?" Trish asked.

"I'm not much of a joiner. And although I had read about it in a few trade mags, I didn't really pay attention. I didn't realize how important the work they're doing is until I met Nic."

"That's interesting," Trish commented.

"You know what's interesting to me?" Chief Rodney asked.

"What, Dad?" his son asked on cue.

"I'm real interested in knowing what a man—what one Leslie Coyne in particular—was doing at a convention of women workers."

The three officers looked at Josie, but she didn't say anything. The same question had occurred to her.

FOURTEEN

JUST WHEN JOSIE thought her summer couldn't get more complicated, Tilly Higgins arrived on the island.

A silver BMW convertible was parked by the curb in front of Island Contractings's office when Josie arrived the next morning. It had been past midnight when Josie finally left the police station, she hadn't slept well, and she was exhausted. Despite the early hour, Tilly Higgins appeared well-rested and full of energy as she leaped out of her car, bounded up the walkway, and started talking before Josie had unlocked her office door.

"You must be Josie Pigeon. Christopher described you, but he didn't mention you were so young!"

Josie suspected that Christopher didn't think of her as young, but she only smiled and offered a conventional greeting.

Mrs. Higgins didn't seem to detect any lack of enthusiasm on Josie's part. "The weather has gotten warm so early this year. New York was absolutely stifling, so I decided I had no choice but to come down here! Besides, I was dying to see how you're getting along. Owning a big family home by the shore has always been one of my dreams. And that it would be designed by my grandson . . . Well, I can't imagine anything better." She stopped, and for a minute a serious expression appeared on her face. "How is dear Christopher working out? I know he has tons of talent," she continued without waiting for an answer to her question. "Dear Christopher has had a bit of trouble in college. He's been known to drink too much and Seymour was very worried last year, but as I told my husband, drinking is so common on college campuses these days and all Christopher needed was something to do. This project has been a godsend," she continued. As Josie fit the key into the lock, Tilly fiddled with the half-dozen gold bangles dangling from each wrist. Tilly was also wearing tight cropped white linen pants, a tiny plaid halter top, and silver sandals. She looked, Josie thought, as though she patronized the same stores as Sam's mother.

"It's so much cooler here. I cannot wait for our new home to be finished so we can move right in."

"There's a lot to be done before that can happen," Josie was quick to point out.

"And that's why I'm here! Dear Christopher said you needed me to make some decisions about kitchen appliances, or cupboards, or something similar," she added.

"I do, but . . ."

"He said you told him you wanted to place orders for these things ASAP."

"Yes, of course. It's just that . . ." Josie stopped and took a deep breath. Her life and this project would be much easier if this woman made these decisions early—and stuck with them. And, fortunately, she didn't seem to know about the murder.

"Of course, I'm sure you're extra busy, what with

these terrible bodies turning up and all, so maybe you could just give me the brochures or Websites or whatever and leave me here to make up my mind. If we're both lucky, I should be done before noon. I have a date for lunch," she explained. Josie, surprised by this development, didn't know what to say. Tilly hadn't finished. "I can assure you that I really do know how to use the Internet," she continued. "My grandchildren made sure of that years ago. And Christopher tells me that the most up-to-date information—catalogues and such—is on line. You do have a high-speed connection, don't you?"

"Yes, of course. I'd be happy to show you the catalogues I have here, and I do have an excellent list of suppliers' sites on the Web as well," Josie added, hoping she could find it. She pushed open the office door and stood back to allow Mrs. Higgins to precede her into the room.

Josie was proud of her office. She felt it exuded the charm of Island Contracting's best work. Over a dozen little houses stood on a shelf that ringed the room near the ceiling, each one a model of a completed Island Contracting project. Visitors to the office for the first time usually commented favorably on the display. Tilly Higgins didn't. She headed straight for Josie's desk at the far end of the room, and much to Josie's surprise, sat down and flipped on the computer.

Josie rushed to join her. She was barely computer literate herself. It had taken her a long time and a lot of work to feel comfortable keeping records in her hard drive instead of on paper, but the last few years of Island Contracting's records were stored in the machine that Tilly Higgins was about to use, and she wanted to make sure they were safe.

Mrs. Higgins seemed to recognize Josie's concerns. "I'm just going to go online and check out some of the Websites Christopher mentioned," she explained, pulling a small leather-bound notebook from her straw purse and flipping through it. "He gave me two lists," she added. "One is the Websites, and one is exactly what I need to decide on now, like whirlpools . . ." She found what she was looking for and frowned. "The dear boy included measurements—I don't suppose they're exact at this stage of the project, though."

"You should come as close to his specifications as possible. He may have designed around certain parameters," Josie suggested, knowing how an inch here and an inch there could add up to disaster.

Tilly sighed and brushed her highlighted hair off her forehead. "Then this may take longer than I had hoped."

"I really need to get over to the . . . to your house," Josie stated.

"Oh, there's no need to stay here with me. Absolutely no need. I'll be fine. I'll just do a bit of research, make a preliminary list for Christopher, and . . ." For the first time, Tilly Higgins seemed unsure of herself. "And I could lock up for you."

Josie didn't have any reason not to trust this woman, but she had no intention of letting anyone else lock her office. "Why don't I come back in two or three hours and see how you're doing. I can lock up if you're done, and you can give me a copy of the items you've picked out."

"And then you can order them! Of course that's the way to do it! Christopher has had nothing but good things to say about you, and now I can see why."

Josie, who had thought some less-than-good things

about Christopher, just smiled. "I have my cell phone with me in case you have any questions or want to leave early. The number is taped to the top of the monitor."

"Good thinking. I'll just call if I need you."

"Great," Josie replied, hoping she would do just that. "And there's an answering machine that will pick up, so don't worry about the phone."

"Of course." Mrs. Higgins was pounding the keys and scrolling down the screen and didn't bother to look up. "Or would you like me to pass on your messages?"

"Thanks, but don't bother. I'll check them when I get back." Josie stuck her hands into the pockets of her overalls and frowned. She didn't feel comfortable leaving Mrs. Higgins there alone, but she didn't see that she had any choice. If she had been going to object, she should have done so immediately. Sunlight gleamed off the heel of Mrs. Higgins's silver shoe and Josie had an inspiration. She paused. "It's possible someone might be stopping by this morning. Carol Birnbaum, my future mother-in-law. She's going to be remodeling the kitchen in her New York apartment, and she wants to look at some of those catalogues too. I hope you don't mind sharing them with her."

"Of course not. I'll just glance through these Websites and she can have all the time she needs with them," Tilly offered generously.

"Great. Then I'll leave you to your task." Josie's cell phone was out of her pocket before the office door swung closed behind her, but she waited until she was in her truck before calling Carol to ask for help babysitting the office. Fortunately, Carol was free and willing, and when Josie explained she was in a hurry, cut short her discussion of possible wedding gowns.

Josie parked her truck in front of the Bride's Secret Bed and Breakfast sign knowing that if Mrs. Higgins were interested in anything other than appliances and fixtures, she would hear about it. She got out, noting that Nic's purple truck was there, as well as Vicki's car and the white Volkswagen beetle with the torn-up fender that Mary Ann drove. Assuming Leslie had come with Vicki, her entire crew was on site nice and early.

Unfortunately, the local police seemed to be there as well. Josie walked by the cruiser, parked behind the Dumpster next to the house, and had to work to resist kicking its shiny side. She just hoped that whatever the Rodneys were there for didn't take too long and didn't involve arresting anyone. With a long list of the possible reasons going through her mind, she was more than a little surprised when she opened the front door and discovered her crew and Trish Petric sharing coffee, doughnuts, and apparently, a joke together. She was even more surprised when the laughter stopped as soon as she entered the room. It was almost as though they felt guilty to be found enjoying themselves—or uncomfortable about whatever had caused so much mirth. Josie put a smile on her face and tried to ignore whatever was going on.

"Hope you left some coffee for me," she said, dropping her tool box on the floor. The crash attracted the attention of everyone in the room, and all with the exception of the police officer were quick to assure her that both coffee and doughnuts were available.

"Leslie even bought the little cream and jelly-filled ones that you like so much," Vicki pointed out.

"That's great," Josie said. She looked at Officer Petric. "Why are you here?" she asked.

"I wanted to check out the crime scene again," Trish Petric answered. "There were a few things that didn't make any sense to me."

"What things?" Josie asked, accepting the Styrofoam cup of coffee that Mary Ann offered with a nod.

"That's police business." Trish's answer was abrupt and in striking contrast to her friendly manner a minute before. "And I've got to get going. More tourists are arriving every day. I have things to do." She slipped off the sawhorse she had been perched on and smiled at the group. "Thanks for the snack. I'll return the favor sometime," she said.

"I'll walk you to your car," Josie spoke up.

"If you don't have anything better to do."

Josie waited until they were together on the sidewalk with the door to the house closed behind them, although she was pretty sure her crew was looking out the wide windows at them, before asking her questions. "Why are you here?"

"I told you. I had some questions about the crime scene. I wanted to look at it again."

"If by the crime scene you mean the place where the body was found, that's upstairs. You were on the first floor laughing with my crew when I arrived."

"I don't know what—if anything—you're implying. But for your information, I had finished upstairs, and when I came back down I was offered coffee and doughnuts. Being hungry, I accepted. Just what are you objecting to?"

"I'm not objecting. You have every right to do what you're doing," Josie answered. "But I have a job to do here, and you're interfering."

"I don't see how that can be true. I made a point of

coming here early. You hadn't even shown up for work. No one on your crew had arrived yet. I . . ."

"How did you get in?" Josie interrupted.

Officer Petric hesitated. "The police department has a key. I assumed you had given it to them . . . to us."

Josie was sure she had done no such thing, but decided this was something to take up with the Rodneys. "You know this is private property."

"I know this is a crime scene and that, if the Rodneys thought it was appropriate, they could prevent you and your crew from working here until our investigation is complete."

Josie had no answer for that so she changed the subject. "You were questioning my crew."

"In the first place, I wasn't doing anything of the kind. We were talking, taking a break. I didn't mention the murder and . . ." She hesitated for just a moment. "And neither did anyone else."

Josie didn't know what else to say. She didn't like this woman being here and talking to her crew, but in truth, she knew she couldn't do anything about it. She didn't like this woman talking to her son either, but again, there seemed to be nothing she could do about it, short of ordering Tyler to avoid her. "I have to get to work" was all she said.

"As do I," Officer Petric answered, "but I may be back."

"I won't hold my breath."

Josie stamped back up the sidewalk knowing she was being irrational and maybe slightly immature. All she was sure of was that this woman irritated the hell out of her and that she didn't trust her one bit.

FIFTEEN

THE CONTINUING DEMOLITION of the upper floors went smoothly. Walls were torn down, warped flooring torn up, closets that had been jury-rigged into odd corners vanished, leaky radiators were pulled out. Early in the morning a large overflowing Dumpster was taken away; an empty one of equal size was delivered within the hour. The new arrival was filled and ready to go before lunchtime. It wasn't until they all sat down to their meal that Josie realized they had been too busy to talk about the murder or a possible arrest. But the topic came up before the first hoagie was unwrapped.

Vicki, who to Josie's knowledge had been working hard ripping up rotten floorboards in the hallway all morning, looked down at her ham and salami on a hard roll and began to sniff. "I can't believe we're sitting here eating lunch when Leslie might be arrested any minute now."

Sitting by her side, Leslie slipped an arm around her shoulder and hugged her. He left a dark handprint on her T-shirt, but they were all so filthy that no one commented—or noticed. "I'm not going to be arrested. I didn't even know the dead guy. Why the hell would I kill him?"

Mary Ann put down her turkey with mayo on white

and looked at him. "I watched this show on Court TV a few nights ago—it was real interesting—all about innocent people who were convicted of crimes they didn't commit. If it weren't for new DNA testing, all of them would still be in prison."

Tears dripped down Vicki's cheeks and onto her lap.

"Not gonna happen to me. My DNA and that dead guy have yet to meet." Leslie took a big bite from his overflowing Italian hoagie and grinned, shredded lettuce falling on the floor.

Vicki jerked away from him. "You're joking around and you should be taking this seriously! You don't know what prison is like."

"I don't, and I'm not going to find out. I didn't kill anyone. No one is going to arrest me for anything. You don't have anything to worry about."

Vicki looked at him and then around the group. "I don't see how you can be so sure."

"No one is going to arrest me because I'm gonna figure out who the murderer is."

Nic looked up from her liverwurst on rye. "Just how will you do that?"

Leslie shrugged. "I don't know right this minute. But the cops on this island don't seem all that smart. It shouldn't be hard to do better than they do."

Josie swallowed a bite of her egg salad on whole wheat before answering. "You're right about that. The Rodneys are idiots, and I'm not sure this new woman is a whole lot better."

"And you've solved murders before, so you'll help me, right?" Leslie continued.

Josie put down her sandwich and looked at him. "How do you know about that?"

"Everyone knows about it. You find a body, you discover the killer—at least that's what was being said in the hardware store the other day when I went in to pick up some new work gloves."

"Yeah, and Mary Ann and I heard the same thing at Sullivan's when we were eating breakfast," Vicki added, perking up a bit.

"Even Officer Petric mentioned it this morning, although I don't think she approved. She sort of suggested that we leave the police business to the police, and they would leave the remodeling to us," Mary Ann explained.

"She didn't sort of suggest, she flat-out said it," Vicki added.

"Do you think that's why she was here?" Josie asked.

Vicki looked puzzled. "I don't know. She was here when Mary Ann and I arrived."

"She and Leslie were sitting on the porch talking when we got here," Mary Ann pointed out.

Leslie picked a thin crescent of hard salami from between the slices of bread and popped it in his mouth. "She was here because of me."

"What do you mean?"

Leslie took a deep breath, his strong shoulders rising and falling, before answering Josie's question. "She was here to warn me . . . about speeding. To tell the truth, I find staying under twenty-five miles an hour a little difficult. Trish has pulled me over a few times."

"A few times?" Mary Ann asked.

"Three."

"No wonder you're on a first-name basis with her," Mary Ann said.

"Yeah. Well, she hasn't given me a ticket yet. She just

came over to tell me that I've gotta get rid of my lead foot."

"She followed you here?" asked Vicki.

"Followed me? I don't think so. She probably just saw my car out front and decided to stop in." He grinned. "Some women just can't seem to get enough of me."

"Les . . ."

"But I'm faithful to the one woman I love," he added, moving closer to Vicki and putting his arm around her.

Josie wasn't about to let the topic die there. "But Mary Ann said that Officer Petric suggested we leave police business to the police, right?"

"Yes, you see, we started talking about the murder—well, we're all thinking about it, right? And she wouldn't answer any questions."

"That's not true," Vicki said. "She answered some of our questions. She told us that the autopsy was complete . . ."

Josie had to interrupt. "Wait a second. Who brought up the murder and who asked the first question? And what was it?" she added.

Leslie's frown matched those on his crew members' faces. "Can't say that I remember exactly."

"I don't either," Mary Ann agreed.

"Now that I think about it, I believe Trish and I were talking about it when you all got here," Leslie said. "I think I brought it up—to change the subject. I asked her if there were any developments since last night or something like that."

"Was she reluctant to tell you anything about the police investigation?" Josie asked.

Leslie frowned. "I don't think so."

"She sure didn't seem reluctant to me," Mary Ann

spoke up. "She was talking about the autopsy in . . . well, in more detail than I was interested in hearing, that's for sure."

"He was stabbed, right?" Josie asked.

"He was stabbed many times," Mary Ann answered, pushing her unfinished sandwich away. "The medical examiner told the police that he . . . he didn't die easily. I think that's how Officer Petric put it."

"Where?"

"Where what?"

"Where was he stabbed? In his chest or in the back?" Josie asked.

"I don't think she mentioned that," Mary Ann said. "Why would it make any difference?"

Josie, who had been watching her share of television shows involving forensics over the last few years, wasn't quite sure why she had asked this particular question.

But Vicki spoke up. "I think if you're stabbed from behind it means you didn't know the person who killed you, but if you were stabbed in the chest, it means you waited for the killer to walk up to you—so you know him, if you know what I mean."

"No, I don't," Nic said. "Why wouldn't someone you know walk up behind you and stab you? And why would the dead person necessarily move away from an unfamiliar person who walks up to them? The knife could have been hidden until the last minute, right?"

"Yeah, but it wasn't a regular knife. It was a mat knife that killed this guy," Leslie pointed out.

Josie hadn't heard that before. "Which sort of directs attention to one of us, doesn't it?"

"I don't see that," Leslie said stubbornly. "Lots of people use those things."

"But I'll bet we all have one in our toolboxes—sort of convenient," Josie answered.

"That's what we should do: We should make sure our tools are in order," Mary Ann said, jumping up. "At least that's what I'm going to do right now. My stuff is upstairs."

"I don't think . . ." Josie began, but Mary Ann was beyond hearing.

"You may as well let her go check out her tools. She won't be comfortable using them until she's satisfied herself that nothing she owns was used to kill that poor guy," Vicki said.

"But there wasn't a weapon found with the body. He must have taken it away with him," Nic said.

"He?" Leslie spoke up. "Exactly why do you think the killer is a man?"

"I don't. I was just talking generally," Nic answered. "Anyway, the killer—he or she—could have used something, cleaned it off, and put it right back in one of our toolboxes. Not that I think he or she did—it would take too much time and effort. If I killed someone on an island, I'd just chuck the murder weapon in the water."

"The tide might bring it right back to the shore," Vicki pointed out.

"Okay. On the bay side of the island then. You could just toss it off one of the public docks. It would land in that muck on the bottom and vanish completely."

"Someone might see you," Vicki pointed out.

"So what? People are always chucking stuff into the bay—crab lines, minnow traps, old bait, shells, whatever. It would be easy to pretend to be crabbing or fishing and get rid of most anything small."

"You seem to have given this a lot of thought. Maybe you're the killer," Leslie said, only half-joking.

Josie stepped in immediately. They had a job to do, and accusations of murder wouldn't make for a congenial workplace. "Look, none of us killed the guy, but that doesn't mean we're not all suspects. The Rodneys aren't bright enough to do a real investigation and I promise you, they would be thrilled to pin this thing on one of us, so we need to stick together and be careful."

"No, it's like I said, we gotta investigate it ourselves," Leslie insisted.

"What we have to do is finish this project on time and on budget," Josie reminded them all. "That's what we're being paid to do. I think we should leave finding the killer to the police and get on with our work."

"Is that an order?" Nic asked.

"I can't stop what you do in your spare time, but I don't want you investigating when you should be working."

Mary Ann appeared in the doorway, a half-smile on her face. "There's someone here."

Josie jumped up immediately. "Who is it?" she asked, wiping her hands on her pants.

"Two women. They're all dressed up like they're going on some sort of fancy cruise or something, but they know you, Josie. The one wearing sunglasses with all these little diamonds on the frames asked if you were busy. I said we were on lunch break, but they just walked right in and started on up the stairs. I didn't know if I should try to stop them or what, but I warned them to watch out—that the floors were torn up and the ceiling was coming down—but they ignored me."

Josie wasn't hanging around to hear more. She knew

the women were Tilly Higgins and her future mother-in-law, but she couldn't imagine why they had shown up here together. And she wasn't going to waste another minute before finding out. Her work boots pounded up the stairs, and she arrived on the second floor in time to see Carol lifting up the yellow police tape so Tilly could duck beneath it and enter the room where the body had been found.

"Carol!"

"Josie, my dear. Lovely to see you." Sam's mother paused long enough to greet her future daughter-in-law before bending down and following the other woman.

Josie didn't hesitate before joining them.

"You'd never know there was a body here just a day ago, would you?" Tilly said, sliding her sunglasses onto the top of her head and peering around.

The room had been cleared of all evidence of the crime. Sunlight was streaming in through the stained-glass windows in the gables onto a decidedly dusty floor. The door hadn't been closed and the residue of ripped Sheetrock, plaster, and horsehair insulation liberally coated everything in the room. Carol pulled her Lilly Pulitzer sweater close about her, but Tilly ignored the filth and leaned against a windowsill to peer out at the street below.

"You really shouldn't be here," Josie protested. "Besides, there's nothing to see, and the police . . ."

"The police on this island are fools. You and I know that, Josie. And I've been explaining the situation to Tilly. She is very concerned."

"There will be no evidence that anything happened here once we're finished," Josie said to reassure her client. "The room is being stripped down to the studs and completely rebuilt. Your grandson has plans for wide window seats in each gable, built-in cabinets along that wall, and double closets at this end of the room."

Tilly Higgins looked around and nodded slowly. "This will be one of three double rooms for the youngest grandchildren," she explained to Carol. "There will be two bunkbeds in each one and lots of storage for games, toys, sports equipment, computers, and all the stuff that kids seem to need these days."

Carol nodded sagely. "We had so much less when we were young," she said.

"Some people still have much less," Josie couldn't resist pointing out.

"True, true," Carol agreed absently, then turned her attention to the other woman. "What do you think?" she asked.

"I think we need to think about this very carefully," Tilly answered seriously. "Dear Seymour was stopped by the island police—for going less than fifteen miles over the speed limit—and he had nothing good to say about them. In fact, if you believe my husband, the police here are incompetent, and I'm afraid he might be concerned about us moving into a home famous for an unsolved murder as well as a ghost."

"The ghost isn't real," Josie protested.

Tilly Higgins opened her eyes wide. "And just how do you know that?"

"Because there isn't any such thing as ghosts," Josie answered.

"But there is a law requiring a Realtor to explain to potential buyers that a house is considered to be haunted," Sam Richardson's deep voice explained.

SIXTEEN

"**T**HERE IS, SAMMY? I had no idea!" Carol Birnbaum said in response to her son's statement.

"This is your son? The lawyer you were telling me about?" Tilly Higgins asked, smiling and looking from mother to son.

"Yes, this is Sammy, my son and Josie's fiancé. As I told you, they're planning a Labor Day wedding and . . ."

"Carol, I don't mean to be rude, but I'm working here," Josie pointed out. She was more than a little disturbed by Sam's appearance—and his statement. "And I don't see why you're here talking about some obsolete law," she continued, scowling at him.

"The law's not obsolete. In fact, it's barely over a decade old," Sam explained.

"Tell us about it," Tilly suggested.

"There are laws in some states—I know New York has one—that require the person selling a house to inform potential buyers of stories or rumors that the home is haunted," Sam explained. "For a Realtor to hide them could quite possibly negate a sale."

"Superstitions and superstitious people," Josie scoffed. "Most buyers know that there's no such thing as ghosts."

"I wouldn't argue with you about that, but whether

or not there are ghosts is not the point. Owners might be inconvenienced by the stories themselves. Workers could refuse to work in a home said to be haunted, for instance, and it's only fair that potential buyers be informed of that possibility."

"I've heard tales of the bride's ghost since I was a teenager, and those stories certainly didn't keep my husband from purchasing this place," Tilly said, but to Josie's ears, she sounded a bit uncertain.

"I've heard those stories too, but I don't believe in ghosts and can't imagine turning down a . . ." Josie floundered, hoping to find exactly the right words. ". . . An excellent job and the chance to create a fine home like the one your grandson has designed just because someone made up a bunch of stupid stories."

"Dear Christopher did joke around about an exorcism," his grandmother admitted. She was frowning.

"I don't think there's any need for that," Sam said. "After all, hundreds, possibly thousands of people have stayed in this house over the years, and no one has seen or heard a ghost."

"Exactly!" Josie beamed at him.

"Then why do we all know the story of the ghost?" Carol asked.

"Whoever owned this place thought the story added to its value." Sam chuckled. "I guess you never picked up one of the brochures touting the bed-and-breakfast. The poor bride's disappearance was prominently displayed on every single piece of promotional material. And there was a large painting of her framed on the wall in the hallway." He looked around. "What happened to that? Did anyone save it?"

"We didn't throw out anything. It's probably either in

the garage or up in the attic. There are still things to be sorted through up there," Josie suggested.

"It would be interesting to see it again," Sam said, and then, turning to Tilly, he changed the subject. "I made reservations for one P.M., not that the restaurant will be crowded at lunchtime, but perhaps we should be going."

Josie's mouth fell open, but not a sound came out. Sam was Tilly Higgins's lunch date? What was going on here? "Where are you two going?" she asked, hoping her question sounded merely casual.

"We're having lunch at the Seagull. Basil's meeting us so we shouldn't be late."

"Why are you lunching on the island?" Josie asked. "I mean, I didn't know you two knew each other." She stopped. She couldn't afford to offend this woman, but she didn't understand what was going on.

"Mother thought that Mrs. Higgins . . ."

"You know I asked you to call me Tilly," Tilly said.

Sam smiled at her before continuing. "Mother thought that Tilly and I might go into business together," he said, smiling at Josie.

There were so many surprises in that sentence that Josie wasn't sure what to ask first. "What sort of business? You're not selling the store, are you?"

"Of course not, I'm just thinking of expanding next year, offering classes in wine and what food goes with what wine. You know the sort of thing."

Actually, Josie didn't. Before she had met Sam, most of the wine she drank came from a box. Most of the food that went with it was pepperoni pizza—with extra garlic. These days Sam either brought something from his store or ordered from the wine list when they ate in restaurants. But she had more questions. "Do you think that sort of thing will be popular here? I mean, do people go on vacation and then take classes?"

Mrs. Higgins leaped in here. "Oh heavens, yes. Why, we know people who take cruises that are really quite intellectual—classes in the morning, island tours in the afternoon. That sort of thing has become very, very popular in the travel industry."

"But here on the island? Sam, you know most people who vacation here just want to lie on the beach, swim in the ocean, fish . . ."

"Perhaps that's because no one has offered anything else," he answered.

Josie frowned. "Yeah, I guess that's possible." She looked over at Mrs. Higgins. "So you're interested in wine, too?"

"Not actually. I'm more concerned with the food. Not that I actually cook anything, but I know a lot about food and wine," she ended.

"So I think she'll be impressed with Basil's place, don't you?" Sam asked Josie.

Josie could tell that he was anxious to leave. "Of course, it all sounds so interesting," she added, making an effort to smile.

"See you tonight," Sam said, kissing the top of Josie's head. "Shall we be off?" he asked Mrs. Higgins.

It seemed to Josie that Tilly was having no trouble smiling up at Sam. Taking the arm he offered, she accompanied him to the door.

They were gone before Josie had time to ask another question.

"I don't think you have to worry about the two of

them, dear. She really is old enough to be his mother," Carol pointed out.

"I . . . that's not it, actually." Josie decided to change the subject. "Do you know if Mrs. Higgins made a list of the fixtures she wants us to install?"

Carol frowned. "She was online going through Website after Website, but I don't know that she actually made any decisions."

"Funny, that's what she said she was going to do." Josie glanced over at her workers. Lunch finished, they were lounging around, chatting, and of course, listening to her conversation. "I have to get back to work, but why don't we go upstairs and look at the room where the body was found again? I could use your opinion about something."

Carol took the hint. "Not to sound ghoulish, but I'd love to see it again."

"We'll get the mirrors off the wall in the butler's pantry," Nic said, standing up and stretching.

"Great. This shouldn't take long. Once we're done there I think we should get to those bathrooms at the back of the house," Josie answered, following Carol up the dusty stairway.

"You thought we needed to be alone for a moment," Carol whispered loudly as she arrived on the second floor landing.

"Yes. Did Tilly do anything other than look at fixtures?"

"Not while I was there, but when I arrived at your office, she wasn't at the computer; she was standing in the back of the room."

"Where the file cabinets are?"

"Exactly!"

"There were some manufacturer's catalogues on top of them."

"But she was looking in a drawer. She closed it as soon as she heard me come in, but I would swear she was going through your files."

"Do you know which drawer?" Josie asked.

"The top one. I'm sure of that. And she didn't want me to know that she was going through it. She slid it shut when she heard me and made some sort of comment about finding it open."

Josie pursed her lips and thought about what Carol was saying. "Did you say anything?"

"Well, I couldn't tell her that I was really there because you wanted me to keep an eye on her, could I? I just introduced myself and asked if she knew where you kept information on sinks and whirlpools. She passed over a few catalogues from the top of the file cabinet. I asked if she had finished with them, and she said that she had, and was going to go check out the Kohler Website. She sat down at your desk and I assume she was doing just that."

"What do you mean? Don't you know what she was doing?"

"Not all the time. The only chair other than your desk chair was on the other side of your desk. I sat down in it because anything else would have seemed odd, but then I realized that there was no way I could tell what she was looking at."

"You're saying you're not sure what Websites she was looking at."

"Yes, so I don't know if she was doing what she had told you she was there to do or not."

"But that's not a problem. I can look at the recent history on my browser and see what Websites were visited today," Josie told her.

"Really? How smart of you to set it up to do that!" Carol beamed at her.

Josie knew this woman would think any woman her son had chosen to marry was the smartest woman in the world, and she hated to disabuse her of this particular falsehood, but she had to explain. "I didn't do anything. It came like that. I think all browsers come like that," she said. "Did you talk to her at all?" Josie asked, knowing the answer. Carol talked to everyone she met, always, period.

"Yes—you know how it is. We chatted about this and that as we looked. She is so excited about this house. Did you know that her husband was buying it for her? I got the impression that he was less enthusiastic about the entire project. You know the young man designing this job is her grandson, don't you?"

"Yes."

"And he went to the same prep school as the grandson of one of my best friends!"

If this fact surprised Carol, it didn't strike Josie the same way. Carol's neighborhood in New York City had always seemed like a small village to her. Everyone appeared to know everyone else at least by reputation if not in actuality. They went to the same schools, shopped in the same stores, ate at the same restaurants, and vacationed at the same resorts. "Christopher seems to be a very nice young man. And so far I haven't discovered any major problems with his plans. Of course, the original structure is sound, so most of his changes are cosmetic."

"Tilly says he's a darling boy, and she's thrilled to be moving into a house he's working on. You know, dear, with the Higginses' connections, this project could end up getting some excellent publicity. You might end up in *The New York Times*—or even *Architectural Digest*!"

"I suppose that would be nice," Josie said unenthusiastically.

"Of course, it is a little late in your career, isn't it? I mean, think what that sort of publicity would have meant to you back when you were struggling to keep Island Contracting in business. Now, of course, things are different—and they're going to be even more different, aren't they?"

"What do you mean?"

"Well, I know how important your work is to you, but it won't be so necessary after you and Sammy tie the knot, will it?"

"You mean I won't have to worry about supporting myself and Tyler."

"You won't have to struggle—that's what I'm trying to say. I know how hard you've worked for so many years without anyone's support. Now you'll have a bigger family, and . . ."

"And Sam's money," Josie said.

"Well, I don't mean to sound crass."

Josie, who had been about to get angry, suddenly realized it was an inappropriate response. Carol thought she was being helpful. "I've had to work hard and there were times when I didn't know how I was going to pay my bills, or give Tyler what he wanted and needed, but I did have support. Risa has let us live in her home and provided us with thousands of meals without making the profit she deserved. A lot of the Realtors on the island have directed their clients to Island Contracting. When things were tough, the hardware store carried Island Contracting on their books without charging any interest. And, of course, my life—and Tyler's—would be completely different if Noel hadn't left me his business and left Tyler the money to go away to boarding school. It's been difficult, but there are a whole lot of people on this island that I owe a lot to."

"Of course, that's one of the reasons your wedding will be so important," Carol said.

"I don't understand. Why would Sam's and my wedding matter to anyone but us, you, Tyler, and a few others?" Josie asked.

"Because, as you've been saying, they all care about you. They've been a big part of your life for years and years. They'll want to celebrate your happiness with you. And I know you'll want to share it with them, too." Carol beamed as though she had just stated the obvious.

And it was obvious, Josie realized. So much for her eloping fantasy.

SEVENTEEN

JOSIE HAD LITTLE time to think about obligations to her friends and colleagues after Carol left. The mirrors on the butler's pantry walls had been difficult and dangerous to remove, and everyone on her crew had spent over an hour dealing with mounds of shattered glass tiles before starting to pull down the false ceiling that had diminished the height of the room. Both jobs were difficult and dirty, and as they worked, Josie began to learn just how irritating her own amateur sleuthing could be to friends and colleagues. After two hours of listening to speculation, inept deductions evolving from incomplete or inaccurate data, and various complex and unlikely theories, Josie claimed to have urgent business back at the office and she left, promising to return within the hour.

She had been busy speculating herself—wondering what a search in her browser's history file would turn up. She flipped on her computer, and in a moment had her answer. Tilly Higgins had apparently been searching for the perfect bathroom fixtures. Period. She turned off the machine and was bending down to pet one of the kittens when she noticed the flashing light on her answering machine. She put the kitten in her lap and pressed the button to replay her message.

Bad news she didn't need, but bad news it was. Her insurance company was threatening to cancel her coverage. Or perhaps the snotty voice was explaining that her coverage had already been canceled. Panicked, Josie grabbed her address book with her right hand and the phone with her left. She found her insurance company's phone number, dialed, and ended up listening to a menu that covered all possibilities. She pressed buttons that indicated her interest in speaking English, in talking about health coverage rather than term life insurance, workman's comprehensive insurance, or long-term care insurance. She waited impatiently after each choice before being offered yet another option. By the time she finally found herself talking to a person, she was frantic and wondering why she had ever stopped smoking.

"May I help you?"

"Yes, I . . ."

"If you will just enter your policy number."

"How?"

"Press the numbers on your phone."

Josie did just that.

"Am I speaking with Arnold Johnson of Johnson Electronics?"

"No. I'm . . ."

"Perhaps you made a mistake. Why don't you enter your policy number again?"

Sighing, Josie did just that.

"Thank you. Am I speaking to Rose Chen of Rose's Nail Salon and Waxing Spa?"

"No. I . . ."

"If you will be more careful perhaps we could try this just one more time."

"Perhaps I could just tell you my policy number," Josie suggested and, before the woman on the other end of the line could protest, she did just that.

"Excuse me while I enter that information."

The line went silent, and for a long moment, Josie was afraid that her suggestion had upset the system so much that she would have to begin again. But the voice returned and Josie finally had an opportunity to ask what their call to her had meant.

"I'm sorry. You pressed the wrong button—you aren't calling about your company's health insurance policy, you're calling in response to our call to you . . ."

"Yes, but your call to me was about my company's health insurance policy," Josie interrupted to point out.

"I understand, ma'am, but that information isn't on my computer. You need to speak to someone in another department."

Josie cursed under her breath.

"Excuse me. I didn't quite hear that, ma'am."

"I was asking if you could transfer my call to someone in that department," Josie lied.

"I would be happy to do that, ma'am. And, if I may suggest that the next time you call us, you listen a bit more carefully to the initial menu offerings."

This time Josie didn't bother to hide her irritation. Before she could finish the one-word curse, she was passed along to the other department.

"Excuse me?"

Josie felt she had no choice but to lie again. "I'm sorry. I spilled some coffee on . . . on my foot. Hot coffee."

"I'm afraid I can't help you with your medical problems, ma'am."

"Don't hang up! Please! I need to talk to you . . . to talk to someone about a message you . . . your company . . . my insurance company . . . left on my answering machine."

"Your name? The name of your company? The number of the insurance policy you wish to discuss?"

Josie answered these questions.

"And you received calls from this office concerning your insurance when?"

"This morning."

"Which call are you responding to?"

"Which call?" Josie glanced at the answering machine. The number five flashed in the little square. The first call had worried her so much that she hadn't even thought of listening to the other five. "The person who called said my company's health insurance policy was in danger of being canceled," she answered, wondering if somewhere in the following calls was one explaining that the first—ha, ha—had been a mistake.

"According to my records, three messages were left on Island Contracting's answering machine this morning."

"I'm afraid I only listened to one of them. The first. The one informing me that my company's health insurance was being canceled. The one that didn't tell me any more than that my company's health insurance was being canceled. The one that did not explain the reason for this particular action. The . . ."

"If you will allow me to explain, Ms. Pigeon."

"Yes, yes, of course. I just . . ."

"We have handled all of Island Contracting's insurance needs for, let me see, I believe for more than three decades. The original owner was a Mr. Noel Roberts. Am I correct?"

"I guess. Yes."

"During that time we have provided health insurance for over five hundred employees."

"That many? Really?"

"Five hundred and nine according to our records."

"Really?"

"Yes and I must remind you that that number does not include dependents."

"You mean relatives."

"Yes, dependent relatives—wives, husbands, children under twenty-one."

"Of course."

"Not of course, Ms Pigeon. I don't know if you realize it, but it is no longer the norm for small companies like Island Contracting to carry health insurance for all of its employees, to say nothing of the employees' dependents. Relatives," she added as though Josie might not understand.

"Island Contracting has always had a policy of taking care of the people who work for it."

"Commendable, but not necessarily practical," the voice on the other end of the line stated.

"I don't see what this has to do with you canceling—trying to cancel—Island Contracting's insurance," Josie said. "After all, my company has always paid its insurance premiums on time." She paused, knowing her statement wasn't absolutely true, and suspecting that the computer screen in front of the person she was speaking with probably was displaying that information. "Very large premiums, too," she added.

"We are not denying that fact. And we are aware that your benefit performance has been exceptional."

"My what?"

"We have not been forced to pay out any large benefits to any of your employees . . . ever, as far as I can tell."

"Which means you've made a lot of money from Island Contracting, right?"

"I don't have those details here."

"But let's assume I'm right and your company has made a large profit from my company. Doesn't that mean your company is obligated to continue insuring it—and my employees? I can't run a business without providing health insurance."

"I don't see why not. More and more companies are doing just that. But that's not the point here."

"No, it's not. I called to find out why your company is canceling my health insurance policy."

"In the first place, if you had listened to all of our calls, you would realize that we are not canceling your insurance. We have raised your premiums and changed your coverage, although I see here that we have been forced to refuse to insure one of your current employees . . . a Miss Leslie Coyne."

"That's a Mr. Leslie Coyne," Josie insisted. "I don't see how you can decide not to insure him when you don't even know his sex."

"We have firm standards. We do not insure people with certain previous conditions . . ."

"I understand that Leslie . . ."

". . . And we have no obligation to continue to insure you for the same premiums forever."

"I . . ." Josie had no idea what to say, then she did. "You will be hearing from my lawyer."

"Naturally, we will respond to all appropriate requests for information, Ms. Pigeon."

"You damn well better," Josie said, slamming down the receiver. Almost immediately, she picked it up and dialed Sam's cell phone. But apparently he had turned it off for his meal with Tilly Higgins. She left a brief "call me immediately" message and hung up. Still furious, she began to pace the room, her work boots loud against the wood floor.

True to her red hair, Josie had a tendency to flare up in anger, but her passion could vanish as quickly as it appeared. The still flashing light on her machine attracted her attention so she sat down, pencil and paper in hand, to listen. The first messages, from her insurance company, caused her to flush with anger again, but she kept on. The next message was from her son. He was going to be busy all afternoon—not to worry, his summer project needed a bit of hands-on work. He would see her at dinner. Josie smiled as she always did when she heard Tyler's voice, but the next message sent her straight back to reality. The call was from the police dispatcher, a woman Josie had known ever since she moved to the island.

"Josie, Chief Rodney wants to talk to you ASAP. He told me to tell you that this is important. To quote him, 'ASAP means ASAP,' whatever that means, but Josie, if you don't call, you'd better avoid running into him. He's really got a bug up his butt this morning. And here he comes . . . I'd better hang up."

The final call was from Island Hardware setting up a delivery of wallboard. Josie made a note on her desk pad to call back and confirm the time as well as the date. Then, sighing deeply, she turned off the machine.

Josie had kept Island Contracting in business through difficult times. She had lived through more than a few murder investigations. But she had never been married, so perhaps it was bridal nerves that caused her to bury her head in her arms on her desk and begin to cry.

Unfortunately, she was still crying when Seymour Higgins entered her office.

EIGHTEEN

"**I** HOPE THE problem you are crying over is personal rather than professional, Ms. Pigeon. I have invited my entire family to celebrate Labor Day in my new beach house, and I assume it will be finished by then."

Josie looked up and, through tears, saw a man wearing a three-piece gray flannel suit—surely the only man so attired on the island on a warm summer day. "Things have been difficult recently," she explained, scrounging in the numerous pockets of her overalls for a Kleenex. She found a wad of dollar bills, some loose change, a broken plastic hair clip, two small Phillips screwdrivers, an old receipt from the local bakery, a handful of shiny brass brads, a lone house key that she didn't dare throw away unidentified, a slip of paper with three phone numbers scribbled on it, a torn tube of dirty wintergreen LifeSavers, and a crumpled coupon for a free cup of coffee at Dunkin Donuts. She tossed the coupon into her wastebasket—the closest franchise was over twenty miles away.

"Here," he said, and Josie realized that she was being offered a monogrammed, hand-hemmed, immaculately pressed linen handkerchief. She looked up at Seymour and smiled. He did not smile back. "Take it. I want to look at the blueprints with you, and I certainly do not want them soiled."

It was either his handkerchief or her sleeve. She took the handkerchief as anger replaced despair. "I'll make an effort to keep my snot to myself," she muttered, sniffling.

"Do that. Now, my dear wife is busy on the island doing something or other, and I want to see exactly what progress has been made at my house."

"We could go over there," she suggested, hoping he would refuse. Years of experience had taught her that owners were usually appalled by the sight of demolition.

"I was just there. Your crew was hard at work."

"They're a good crew," Josie said, pleased that he had noticed—and relieved that they hadn't happened to be on a break when he arrived.

"They're paid to work and they were working. I wouldn't have expected anything less. And I hope you don't either."

"I hire good people," she said stubbornly.

He chose to ignore her comment. "I want to make sure Christopher has incorporated enough closet space in his design, especially in the master suite. My dear wife can't imagine a week going by without at least one trip to Bergdorf's or Saks. And everything that's not on her back must be warehoused—preferably out of my sight."

Josie got up, walked over to the large cabinet where blues were stored and pulled out the plans for the Higgins's house. She doubted if he was impressed with her efficiency, but she was. She unrolled the papers across her messy desk.

"You need a large table to lay these out on."

Josie looked around her small cozy office. "There isn't a whole lot of room here."

"And you should get rid of those stupid birdhouses. They probably collect dust and they give the wrong impression to potential employers."

"I don't see why."

"Who wants to hire a builder who builds bird-houses?"

"Those aren't just birdhouses. They are also replicas of houses that Island Contracting has either remodeled or built."

"Really?"

He didn't even bother to glance up at them, Josie noticed. "Really," she answered firmly.

"You have done a lot of work, haven't you?"

"Yes." She was shuffling through the blues. "The closets in the master suite could be enlarged if they extended into the room a bit . . ."

"No, I like a lot of room. How about breaking through into the room behind them and appropriating some of that space?"

Josie frowned. "That's possible, of course, but that particular room is already fairly small. See, there are three other suites—smaller than the master, of course—on that floor. We could, of course, make one even smaller . . ."

"Let's try that. We can always give that suite to my youngest granddaughter and her husband—can't stand the guy—and maybe living together in close quarters will encourage them to get divorced. She's still young enough to find another husband, especially with the possibility of a large inheritance looming in her future." That settled, Seymour made himself at home in Josie's desk chair.

Josie was still staring at the blues. "I should run this by Christopher."

"You do that. If he gives you any argument, tell him to remember who's paying the bill for this damn thing. *Achoo!*"

"Bless you." Josie looked over at her employer as he sneezed again. His eyes were watering and, as she watched, a large red hive appeared on his forehead.

"What the . . ." he roared, waking up the pair of kittens that had been sleeping underneath the desk. The little gold tabbies moved to the middle of the floor and stretched. "What the hell are those cats doing in here? I'm allergic to cats!" he yelled, leaping away from the animals as a series of sneezes filled the room.

"Then you may need this," Josie said, handing him his handkerchief, now crumpled and filthy.

Josie was not in the mood for a festive family gathering, but she didn't seem to be able to avoid this one. Sam appeared in the early afternoon to explain that his mother was making one of her specialties, and wanted to know if Josie was coming to dinner. Claiming a problem at his store, he left before Josie could think of a reason to spend the evening at home, or tell him about her meeting with Seymour Higgins, or ask about his lunch with Tilly. Then Risa left a message on her cell phone explaining that she had been asked to dinner and was bringing her shellfish risotto. Josie was still hoping to opt out of the evening when Tyler called and asked her to pick him up and take her to Sam's for dinner. She still would rather be alone to think through her various problems, but an opportunity to be with her son wasn't something she was going to miss.

But first she had to talk to her crew. She considered picking up a six pack of Coors Light, a bottle of wine— anything to deaden the blow—but finally, she decided to just explain the situation and see how everyone reacted. More important, she had to see if she actually had a crew after they were told that in a few weeks, they might no longer be insured.

"I can and I will, of course, protest their decision and I'll certainly look for another insurance company," she explained, "but . . . to tell you the truth, I don't know if anyone will offer a policy that Island Contracting can afford. I honestly have no idea what is going to happen."

Nic was the first to speak up. "Oh well, life's like that," she said, leaning down to retie a loose bootlace.

"Yeah," Mary Ann agreed, getting up from where she had been sitting and unbuckling her tool belt. "Who's gonna stop at the bakery tomorrow morning?"

"Leslie and I will," Vickie volunteered.

"Yeah, and I can guarantee that all you beautiful ladies will get some bear paws," he added.

Josie was astounded by their reaction. "I . . . I don't think you understand. I promised you all benefits when I hired you. Now it's possible that you won't have health insurance."

"Yeah, we get it," Nic said, looking up. "And we get that it's not your fault. Stupid insurance company is trying to screw you."

"And us," Leslie pointed out.

"Yeah, and us. So you'll fight back and maybe you'll win and maybe you won't. But I'm in good health and this is a good job. I think I'll stay on," Nic said.

"Me too," Mary Ann agreed.

"We're with you," Vicki said looking at Leslie.

"Yeah," he agreed. "After all, I seem to have fallen into the uninsured group anyway." A crooked grin appeared on his face. "Do you think I'll get free medical care if I'm arrested?"

"You're not going to be arrested!" Vicki cried.

"Of course you're not," Josie said. "Listen, Sam's mother is cooking dinner and I need to shower and change, so I'd better hit the road."

"One of us can lock up," Vicki offered.

"Great." Josie passed over the key, and after some discussion of the next day's work, hit the road. But on the way home she made an important decision: she would spend her personal nest egg on the inflated insurance premium. She couldn't change Leslie's situation, but she could keep Island Contracting's unspoken contract with its workers. She would make sure they were taken care of.

Dinner was a disaster.

Josie arrived late. And, by the time she arrived, Risa and Carol were barely speaking to each other and Sam had retreated to his computer screen claiming an urgent need to "check something out." Then Tyler left early, explaining that he had an appointment.

"What sort of appointment?" Josie asked.

"I don't believe he said who he was meeting, but I'm sure it has to do with that school project he keeps talking about," Carol explained, picking up a wooden spoon and stirring the steaming contents of a large pot simmering on the stove.

"My risotto, learned at Mama's knee, cannot be left for a moment. That the way the Italians do it," Risa said.

"My risotto, which I learned to make from one of the most famous chefs in the world, must be eaten as soon as it is prepared." Carol looked over at the heavy pottery casserole sitting in the middle of Sam's nineteen-fifties kitchen table.

"You both made risotto?" Josie asked.

"We both made seafood risotto," Carol corrected her.

"We see which you and Sam like most—for your wedding party," Risa explained.

"Oh . . . ah, I think I hear Sam calling me," Josie said. If these two strong-minded women were feuding, she sure wasn't going to get caught in the crossfire. Besides, she could use an explanation from Sam, and she demanded one.

"What the hell is going on in your kitchen?" she asked, appearing in Sam's small study and flopping down in one of the Eames chairs he valued so highly.

"Lord, it's a mess, isn't it?"

"Yes, but how did they happen to make the same thing? Carol doesn't usually make Italian dishes. I was expecting her smothered brisket or rolled flank steak."

"This is all my fault. I was on the phone with Mom last week, and I just happened to mention that you loved seafood risotto and were hoping to serve it at our reception. Apparently she thought I was asking her to cook."

"You're kidding! I practically promised Risa that she could cook for the reception. You know, Sam, she's been helping me raise Tyler since his birth."

"I wish I were kidding. You know, Josie, if we just firm up our plans we'll be able to tell everyone what's going to happen, and this type of thing will just be a bad memory."

"Sam, I will. It's just that there's so much happening

that I don't have much time to think about the wedding. I mean, it's going to be in September, and right now I have more immediate problems. Not more important," she added, seeing the beginning of a frown appear in his face. "More immediate."

"I sort of hoped that you wouldn't think of our marriage as a problem," Sam said softly, turning back to his computer.

"I . . . it's just the wedding, not our marriage. I don't think of it like that at all. She leaned over his shoulder and stared at the screen. "Ghosts?"

"I was doing a little research about your problem."

"My problem?"

"Yes. The Bride's Secret Bed and Breakfast ghost. It's pretty well known. I found it mentioned on more than one Website about supernatural events in this state."

"Really?"

"Yes. But that's not what's interesting. The ramifications of a known ghost are amazing. There was actually a case in New Mexico where an insurance company refused to insure anyone working in a building the ghost of an Anasazi child is said to inhabit. Stupid, but a disaster for the company located there, of course," he said scrolling down the screen.

"Isn't disaster a little strong?" she asked. "I mean, maybe the workers would work without insurance."

"They might, but the owner of the company would be liable if something tragic happened to one of them."

"Even if the owner couldn't get—or afford—insurance?"

"Sure. And there was a case in San Francisco of a ghost said to inhabit an elevator in a warehouse that was scheduled to be turned into condos. The liability question was such that the owner finally tore down the building and sold the land to a developer for a parking garage. I haven't been able to find out if the garage has a ghost," he added, continuing to scroll.

Josie might not be able to make decisions about their wedding, but she decided on the spot to keep Island Contracting's insurance problems to herself.

NINETEEN

JOSIE WAS ALMOST always optimistic when she woke up. The sea air coming through her open bedroom window was fresh and sweet smelling. After a night's rest, her back no longer ached from the previous day's exertion. Work that she loved was waiting to be done. She would see the man she loved . . . and then she remembered the events of the previous day: the visits of both Mr. and Mrs. Higgins, the calls from her insurance company, the unsolved murder, Risa and Carol's risotto competition, and Sam's comments about their wedding.

She sat up in bed, all remaining shreds of optimism vanishing as she remembered her son's unexplained behavior the night before. Everything had started out as usual. His arrival had been greeted with enthusiasm by Risa and Carol; each had plied him with risotto demanding, not too subtly, to know if hers was the best. Tyler had been busy eating and tactfully responding to their pressure when Sam brought up his senior project. Tyler had changed the subject to his summer job. Then Carol mentioned seeing him talking with the new woman police officer. Josie couldn't ignore that, but when she questioned him, Tyler had refused to answer, making a joke about older women. Tyler had been raised to be honest and forthright. The night before he had been neither. His one word answer ("around") to her inquiry of where he had been all afternoon was only slightly shorter than his explanation for what he had been doing ("not much"). Usually voluble, Tyler's reticence had worried Josie until she fell asleep.

Now Urchin, Tyler's Burmese cat, wandered into the room as Josie swung her feet to the floor. She frowned. Urchin preferred her son's company and usually remained by his side or in his lap when he was home. If Urchin was here, Tyler probably wasn't. Pulling on a ragged flannel robe, she followed the cat back to the room that served as living room, dining room, and kitchen in her small apartment. The open door to her son's bedroom revealed only his unmade bed.

"Tyler?"

Urchin meowed by her feet and Josie frowned. Tyler wasn't expected at work until nine—where had he gone? Years before they had developed a system of communicating through messages left on the worn chalkboard hanging near the stove, but the board revealed only the shortage of eggs and mustard in the refrigerator. Josie headed back to her bedroom to get dressed. The previous night's dinner had been delicious and filling, but she had a lot of hard work ahead of her. A trip to Sullivan's was in order.

On the drive to the north end of the island where Sullivan's was located, she decided it was time to take control of the situation. Her son had given her a little notebook that was attached to her truck's dashboard, and she ripped off the top sheet, taking a moment to wonder if they could really be out of ketchup as well as mustard. She found a tiny pencil someone had brought from an Atlantic City casino, and prepared to get organized. She would make a list, which would focus her mind as she ate.

But it was, Josie realized, impossible to focus on one thing when surrounded by people interested in discussing something else. Of the dozen or so diners sitting in the small luncheon area of Sullivan's, ten had opinions about either the murder, the ghost at the Bride's Secret Bed and Breakfast, or some aspect of Josie's upcoming nuptials. By the time her breakfast had arrived at her table, Josie was more confused than ever.

Her young waitress stopped to chat after delivering her meal. "I was talking to Tyler and he said you haven't bought your wedding dress yet. Is that true? I'm going to wear something long, white, and silky," she added, apparently thinking it was an unusual concept. "And I'm going to buy it in New York City! There are stores on Madison Avenue where the most beautiful wedding dresses in the world are made—at least that's what I've heard."

Josie was momentarily taken aback by the realization that girls her son's age were dreaming about weddings; then she had a small epiphany. "You would go all that way to buy your wedding dress? Really?"

"Of course, it's the most important day of your life, you know."

"Yeah, but . . ."

"I told Tyler that, and he said that you would never go so far. He said he didn't think you were that interested in being a bride, and that you'd probably get married in something you bought right here on the island."

"Tyler doesn't think I'm interested in being a bride?" Josie repeated "Really? He said that?"

"Yes, and I told him . . ."

"You know what?" Josie asked, putting her napkin in her lap. "I've been thinking about it, and Tyler is wrong. I am going to go to New York City!"

"How romantic!" the waitress gushed. A shout from the cook recalled the girl to her job, and Jose was left alone with her meal. Josie picked up her fork, stabbed the egg on her plate, and watched as the yolk ran into the pile of bacon strips. "And, who knows, I may even get around to looking at wedding gowns," she muttered, finishing her thought as she stuffed an overflowing fork into her mouth.

Normally a fast eater, Josie polished off her breakfast in record time. She left a large tip, since unintentional good advice could be as valuable as a well-considered suggestion, and hurried back to her truck. She couldn't leave the island until she had talked to a few people.

She hadn't been sure how her workers would feel about her sudden departure, but they all seemed perfectly happy to continue to work on their own. Sam, though surprised, was happy when she explained that she was going to be shopping for a wedding gown—he even offered her a sheet of directions from the island to Manhattan that he had made for his mother to use on her frequent trips back and forth. Josie tucked the page into her jeans, kissed him good-bye, and hurried to her apartment. The thought of leaving without seeing Tyler caused her some momentary qualms, but Risa, also thrilled with the thought of her wedding gown shopping, promised to feed and care for Tyler until she returned.

And it was not as though she was going to be gone for long, Josie reminded herself, changing into the one pair of black slacks that she owned. With a clean white shirt and black leather sandals, she felt she was properly dressed for her task. She wound the three gold mesh bracelets Sam had given her for Christmas around her wrist and noted the sparkle of her large diamond engagement ring. Pausing only for a trip to the local ATM, Josie was off the island and on the highway in record time.

Her optimistic view of what she was doing lasted for almost fifty miles. The next hundred miles were haunted by doubt. By the time she was stuck in a traffic jam in the middle of the George Washington Bridge, she would have turned around and run home, if only she could have. By the time she arrived at Betty and Jon's Upper East Side apartment lobby, she was starving, tired, and wishing someone else had waited on her at Sullivan's. She had called Betty from the road and the doorman was expecting her. He explained that Betty was waiting in her apartment. "Go on up. Fourteen E. The elevator's to your right."

Josie followed his directions and was immediately reminded of the fondness elevator designers had for mirrored walls. Her disheveled appearance was reflected and multiplied over and over. Her clothing, which had seemed simple and sophisticated at home, looked simplistic and wrinkled here. Her hair could use washing and the skin on her nose was peeling. She refused to consider her fingernails.

She forgot all of this when the door of Fourteen E opened and her best friend flew into her arms.

"Josie!"

"Betty!"

"Mommmeeeee!"

The last was wailed from inside Betty's apartment.

Betty laughed and pulled Josie through the door. "Come on in. JJ's going through a dependent stage, poor dear. I have to be in sight constantly. But he's ready to go with us," Betty continued, pointing to the plush stroller where JJ Jacobs sat waving a Ziploc bag stuffed full of Cheerios. As Josie approached, his fat face wrinkled up and tears began to drip down his chubby cheeks.

"He's afraid of strangers—it's just a phase and I'm sure he'll love you as soon as he gets to know you." She turned to Josie. "Do you have to use the bathroom before we go?"

"Go where?"

"To buy your wedding gown."

"How do you know about that?" Josie was mystified.

"Let's see, Risa called right after you did. She said to tell you that Tyler is spending the night with Sam and Carol and that you should not worry about feeding Urchin. And she suggested that with your hair color cream might look better than pure white." Betty stood back and examined her friend from head to toe. "Risa has great taste and, you know, she's probably right."

"But . . ."

"Then Carol called. She wanted you to know that Tyler can stay with Sam all week long if you want and that you shouldn't hurry back."

Betty pulled a long list from a large quilted bag sitting on a nearby chair. "She also wanted to make sure we go to the right stores—she actually knows the personal shoppers at Saks, Bergdorf's, and Bendel's, although she suggests we try a small boutique about six blocks from here on Lexington as well."

"She probably knows at least one person at every boutique on the Upper East Side," Josie muttered.

Betty grinned. "That does sound like her. I was thinking we should start up at Vera Wang's, but maybe we should go to the place Carol suggests instead."

"But I . . ." Josie didn't finish yet again. Betty flung her arms around her neck again and gave her a hug.

"I can't tell you how happy I am that you're here to buy your dress. I've been feeling, well, sort of left out. My life here is wonderful, but I miss the island, and being an important part of planning your wedding is almost like being back there for a bit. How long can you stay?"

"I really have to get back to work. You know how it is. The job we're on is huge. Remember the Bride's Secret Bed and Breakfast? It's being turned into a private home."

"And Island Contracting has the job! That's wonderful! You're going to have to tell me all about it."

"So I can't stay here for more than a day. But I do have to use the bathroom," Josie said.

"Oh, you've been on the road for hours—of course! That door right there, and be sure to check out the sink. It's the latest thing."

Josie rushed into the small room and closed the door behind her. Buying a wedding gown had only been her excuse to come to New York. She had really come to the city hoping to talk to Jon Jacobs about her insurance situation. Jon, a criminal lawyer and good friend of Sam's, might have a solution to her problem. She had thought they might talk, he would make a few calls, and then she would go back home. She realized now that her plan had been completely unrealistic. She should have stayed home working with her crew instead of standing in her oldest friend's bathroom preparing to disappoint her.

Josie looked at herself in the mirror and frowned. Sam had said they were obligated to include their friends in their happiness, and she knew Betty would adore helping her look for a dress. It wasn't as if they had to actually buy one. In fact, if Carol was right, wedding dresses took months and months to manufacture, so there was no way Josie would be able to buy one here anyway. Josie pulled her shoulders back and smiled at herself. She would give Betty this shopping trip, spend the night if she must, and get up early the next day and drive home. Surely the traffic would be light in the early hours of the morning. She could probably make the trip in half the time it had taken her to arrive. Having a plan, she turned and opened the door.

Betty and JJ were waiting. The broad smile on Betty's face made Josie glad of her decision. She chose to ignore JJ's scowl.

"Where do we go first? Saks?" Josie had become familiar with the huge edifice on Fifth Avenue the winter before when Carol had dragged her through department after department trying to get her wardrobe in shape for a New York City winter. At least she would feel at home there.

"I suppose . . ." Betty sounded reluctant.

"And you mentioned Vera Wang." If Josie was doing this for her friend, she was determined to get it right.

"They're the most beautiful dresses in the world, but they're sort of expensive." Betty pulled her son's fist from his mouth before asking a question. "You're not paying for the dress yourself, are you?"

"Of course I am!" Josie maintained, although her nest egg had vanished.

"I got the impression from Carol that price was no

object. I assumed that meant that Sam—or Carol—was paying for it." The phone on the tiny table in the hallway rang, and Betty answered it, explaining to the person on the other end of the line that she was busy.

Josie sighed and bent down to JJ's level. He had fallen asleep in his stroller, his head lolling against the padded back. She touched his soft skin with one fingertip, and he opened his eyes and stared at her, a serious expression on his chubby face.

"Well, that's settled," Betty said, hanging up. "So let's get going and find you a dress. If you make your choice quickly, maybe we'll have time to shop for mine."

"Your what?"

"My dress for your wedding. You are here to ask me to be your maid of honor, aren't you?"

JJ began to scream. Josie smiled at the child. She knew exactly how he was feeling.

TWENTY

IF SHE WAS doing this for all the years of Betty's friendship, she was going to do it right, Josie decided. They began at Saks, then moved up and across the street to Bendel's and Bergdorf's. The white dresses washed out her pale complexion, and her muscular arms were not made to be exposed above layers of tulle and lace. At least her chunky legs were hidden by the long skirts. Then, just as Josie was feeling fatter and poorer than she had ever felt in her life, they left Fifth and started up Madison. Josie was tired and hungry, but Betty was on a quest and seemed to have unlimited energy. Just when Josie thought her feet were going to fall off, JJ began to scream again. Betty responded immediately.

"That means he's hungry. There's a great little Italian place just around the corner a few blocks up. Let's go there. JJ loves panini."

Josie didn't even know what panini were, but she was starving. "Great idea. Poor kid," she added as an afterthought.

JJ sobbed until they turned the corner and the café came into view. "He loves to eat here," Betty explained. "I just hope they're not too busy."

"Boy, when you said little, you meant little," Josie

said, peering into the restaurant. Tables were jammed together leaving little space for customers or waiters to pass, but fortunately, as they arrived two women got up from one of the trio of tiny tables set up on the sidewalk. Betty, showing her skills as an adopted New Yorker, wheeled her son over and sat down, staking her claim on the spot.

Josie dropped onto the remaining chair as Betty undid the straps keeping her son in his stroller and lifted him onto her lap. "So what do you think?" she asked Josie, smoothing JJ's hair.

"It looks nice, but I haven't seen a menu."

"I mean the gowns. Which one did you like best? I loved the last one you tried on at Saks. You know, Risa had a point. You do look better in ivory than pure white. And that drop waistline and the full skirt really made you look thin."

"Betty, it was over eight thousand dollars! I can't afford anything like that! You know how I live."

"But I thought Sam . . ."

"Sam would pay for anything I ask him to pay for, but I really don't want to start our marriage asking him to splurge on a dress I'll only wear once. I'm not like that! It's just not like me."

"What do you want to eat?" Betty asked. "The salads are excellent, and the panini, of course."

Josie had a feeling that Betty was intentionally changing the subject. "Whatever JJ's having," she answered sullenly. "And coffee."

"Espresso or cappuccino? Low fat or decaf?" A skinny waitress wearing black pants, a white shirt, and looking exceptionally chic appeared at their table.

Betty placed their order with Josie explaining that

"regular old American coffee" was just fine with her, and the young woman took off.

"She looks better in her outfit than I do," Josie said, watching their waitress slip through the small space between tables with ease.

"She didn't get up early this morning, drive almost two hundred miles, and then spend two hours trying on wedding dresses," Betty reminded her.

Josie just smiled.

While Betty and JJ enjoyed playing a game of "Where's JJ?" with a large linen napkin, Josie looked around. In the city the winter before, the many fur coats on the street had amazed her. Now, relieved of their bulky furs, these women were universally thin. Josie, starving, wondered if they had come to the right place for their late lunch. Her doubts vanished when three huge platters of food appeared before them. Panini turned out to be the grilled sandwiches Risa had been feeding her for years. The one Betty had ordered for her was stuffed with two cheeses, grilled peppers, pesto, and leaves of fresh basil. "JJ eats pesto?" Josie asked after swallowing her first delicious bite.

"Loves it. I give him the cheese and pesto here—he can't handle the bread yet—but at home I put it on pastina, and he just wolfs it down."

Josie had begun to feel better and she smiled down at the child, now back in his stroller. "Risa would love to hear that. When Tyler was a baby she used to say that children need pasta each day—and she made sure he got it too."

"How is Risa?" Betty asked, picking up her fork and stabbing a tiny tomato on top of her salad.

It was a long lunch and Josie spent much of it catching Betty up on island matters. By the time they were sipping the dregs of their coffee and JJ had fallen into a deep sleep, Josie was feeling better and was willing to look at a few more wedding dresses.

"The place Carol called about is nearby," Betty said.

"Then we'd better go there first. Did you say she gave you the name of someone there?"

Betty smiled. "Gertrude Weintraub. And you're in for it. Carol described Gertrude as someone who can find the perfect dress for anyone. And she was going to call and tell her that we were on the way."

Josie closed her eyes. "I have a feeling I'm being set up for ruffles and a train—something like Princess Diana's wedding dress."

"I think that would be a mistake—even for someone as young and beautiful as she was," Betty said, getting up.

"And I'm neither." Josie sighed, straightened up, and smiled at her good friend. "Okay, let's go."

The place Sam's mother had recommended was up a flight from the street. There was an elevator, but while Betty and JJ waited for it, Josie took the stairs.

She entered a white world of beading, Swarovski crystals, lace, silk, and ruffles. If trying to explain the action to Carol wouldn't have been more daunting than staying, Josie would have fled immediately.

A wave of white brocade parted and a short, blue-haired, chubby woman appeared. "Josie Pigeon."

"Gertrude Weintraub?"

"Got it in one, my dear. Although everyone calls me Gert." She peered behind Josie. "Didn't dear Carol say you would have a friend with you? And a baby?"

"Yes, they're waiting for the elevator. The baby is

sleeping and his mother—my friend Betty—didn't want to take him out of his stroller and risk waking him up."

Gert beamed. "Lovely. To tell you the truth, I was a tiny bit worried. This is no place for children—sticky fingers can make such a mess of my skirts."

Josie realized Gert was talking about the wedding gowns lining the walls and stuffed on racks, not the sensible black cotton skirt she herself wore. "I'm sure. But you don't have to worry about JJ—he's a sweetheart."

"Sweetheart or no, I've set up a playpen full of toys in my office for him. So many women are getting married more than once these days, and so many bring their children to fittings, that I've become accustomed to taking care of the dear little heirs while their mothers shop."

Just then JJ and Betty appeared. JJ was still asleep, and Betty rolled him into a corner where he couldn't do any damage when he woke up. Then she introduced herself to Gert. Josie wandered around, fingering thick embroidered and beaded silk, touching feathery layers of chiffon, putting her hands behind her back when she discovered what looked like handmade lace. She couldn't imagine herself in anything she saw, but she was ready to endure whatever Gert offered—for Carol's sake.

She was becoming depressed over the prospect when Gert left Betty and appeared by her side. "I already pulled out a few dresses after dear Carol described you and your life. She seemed to have little idea of what sort of wedding you wanted, whether something casual at the beach, a church wedding, or possibly something small in a private home. So I picked out one for each. And two dresses that are my favorites—I couldn't resist. They're waiting in the dressing room back there." Josie took a deep breath and, steeled for the worst, headed toward the white curtain offering privacy from the rest of the room. At least no one would be able to see the expression on her face when she looked in the mirror.

As promised, there were five dresses waiting for her. Josie approached them slowly. All were the color she had learned this morning to refer to as ivory (at Saks the word *beige* had been roundly scorned). Three were full-length, one had a handkerchief hem, and one, surprisingly, was a tailored suit with a fitted jacket and knee-length skirt. She decided to try the suit on first.

A few minutes later, she was standing before the bank of mirrors, absolutely amazed by her appearance. The suit was transforming. She looked wonderful—fashionable, and if not thin, appealingly curvaceous. She pushed aside the curtain and rejoined the others.

"Fantastic! Josie, that suit is fantastic!"

"But only appropriate if you're going to be married in a private home, or perhaps before a judge at City Hall. You need to try on the others as well, my dear," Gert suggested firmly.

"We could get married at Sam's house," Josie said, turning around in front of the mirror.

"Perhaps," Gert said. "Now I think we should skip the gown with the handkerchief hem. I hadn't met you when I picked that one out, and it really won't do at all. Try on the floor-length sheath with the little bolero jacket next. That will do for a beach wedding without the jacket and a church wedding with it."

Josie did as she was told—repeatedly—and in slightly over an hour or so, she had chosen three dresses that she actually loved. "So which is it?" Betty asked when Josie reappeared in her street clothes.

"I . . . I really don't know." Gert was leaning over the

playpen and patting JJ on his back. "There aren't any price tags," she whispered.

Apparently she didn't whisper quietly enough. "You don't have to worry about the cost, my dear," said Gert. "Carol said to assure you that the gown you love is her present to you. Such a dear woman."

"But I . . ."

"Pick the one you like and I'll have it ready for you on the big day."

Betty and Gert were smiling expectantly. Josie looked from dress to dress, completely undecided. "I . . . is there a ladies' room?"

Gert pointed. "That door to your right."

"Thank you." Josie fled toward a few minutes of privacy, leaving Betty and Gert behind, happily discussing veils versus hats. As she closed the door behind her, the subject of flowers came up. It was all too much.

Josie flipped down the toilet seat lid and sat. She needed to think. She was losing control of her life. She hadn't really come to the city to shop, anyway. The wedding dress had been an excuse to see Betty, and to talk her into asking her husband for help. Now here she was, being forced to choose between dresses, which meant that she had to decide on the spot what sort of wedding she and Sam were going to have. Dresses she couldn't possibly afford. Dresses she was not going to allow anyone else to buy for her. She was further than ever from getting what she had driven so far for.

She looked over at the pile of magazines and newspapers laid out on the windowsill and recognized a name in a headline. She picked up the yellowing newspaper and returned to the salon.

"Betty, how well do you know your neighbors?"

"Some well, some not at all."

"How about Maud Higgins?" Josie asked. "It says here that she lives in your building."

"Oh, I know Maud. She has a daughter the same age as JJ. We meet in the park sometimes, and we're talking about forming a play group for the kids before winter comes."

"You know Maud Higgins?" Gert spoke up. "I sold her her wedding dress. A dear young woman with a lovely, willowy figure. She chose the most gorgeous Edwardian sheath in the palest, palest pink, and she carried cream tulips with just a hint of blush in the center of each flower. Beautiful."

Josie smiled. New York City was really just a group of small neighborhoods. Maybe this trip wasn't going to be a waste of time after all.

TWENTY-ONE

"**S**HE WAS A lovely bride," Gert said, looking over Josie's shoulder at the magazine she held. "But did she decide to use Higgins instead of her husband's name?"

"She's still married," Betty answered the unasked question. "She uses Higgins because that's how she's known professionally."

"What does she do?" Josie asked.

"Right now she's a stay-at-home mom, but before her daughter was born she was a magazine editor. She worked everywhere—*Harpers, Vogue, Elle*—as well as a bunch of smaller magazines."

"That's right. She was such fun to help find a wedding gown. She knew wonderful stories—things that happened backstage at Bryant Park during Fashion Week, the fall shows of the really big designers in Paris, all sorts of lovely things." Gert smiled at the memory.

"And she's the granddaughter of Seymour and Tilly Higgins?" Josie asked, wanting to be sure of her facts.

"Yes," Betty answered.

"No," Gert protested. "Or perhaps I should say not exactly. Seymour Higgins is her grandfather, yes. But the present Mrs. Higgins—Tilly Higgins—isn't her biological grandmother. Her biological grandmother is the first Mrs. Higgins. I seem to remember that her first name was Doris."

"I didn't know he was married more than once," Josie said.

"Are you working with the trophy wife then?" Betty asked.

"She seems a little old to be a trophy wife," Josie answered.

"How old is she?" Betty asked.

"It's not how old she is that makes her a trophy wife, it's the difference in their ages," Gert explained. "And trophy wife or no, the second Mrs. Higgins has had that title for well over three decades. I haven't had the pleasure of meeting Seymour or Tilly but they're forever appearing in photographs in the paper at various charity dos and benefits."

"So this isn't the story of a rich older man and a beautiful younger wife," Josie said.

"Not at all," Gert said. "In fact, the present Mrs. Higgins is at least as wealthy as her husband. Her family was in insurance—one of the big companies located up in Hartford. They were loaded and she was an only child. And she raised Seymour's children as though they were her own. I think there were four: one boy and three girls. Maud Higgins is his son's daughter. The two youngest girls bought their wedding gowns from me decades ago, as have their daughters."

"What about the third daughter?" Josie asked.

"Bergdorf's," Gert answered dismissively. "The marriage only lasted a few years. She took off with another man and moved to California."

Josie got the impression that Gert didn't think this

would have happened if the bride had more carefully chosen her shopping venue.

"What happened to Maud's biological grandmother? To Doris? Did she die?" Betty asked.

Gert walked over to a manikin and straightened the lace hem of the gown on display as she answered. "I seem to remember that she fell in love with another man and ran away from her family. And then she died under unusual circumstances. I can't say I remember the details, if I ever knew them. It was all something of a mystery." She removed the veil and, cradling the yards of lace and silk in her arms, disappeared into the dressing room.

"That's odd, isn't it?" Betty asked Josie.

"What's odd?"

"A bride vanishing like that. It's sort of like the story of the Bride's Secret Bed and Breakfast come to life."

"If she had four children before leaving, she wasn't exactly a bride," Josie mused. "It is odd, though. But that's not what interests me."

"What is?"

"Tilly and Seymour knew the Bride's Secret when they were young—before he was married to his first wife."

"So?"

"So it's interesting that they ended up buying it together decades later, isn't it?"

"Do you think it has anything to do with the murder?"

"Probably not."

"Could the body you found be his first wife?" Betty asked.

"Not unless his first wife was a man," Josie reminded her.

Betty laughed before asking another question. "And there's no reason to connect the murder with anyone in the Higgins family, right?"

"Just that they own the house where it happened."

"And no one has identified him?"

"No. Fingerprints were taken and I suppose someone somewhere is trying to find a match, but I haven't heard anything." Josie paused. "Did I tell you that Leslie Coyne—he's the electrician on the crew this summer— that his papers were found on the body?"

"What sort of papers?"

"His driver's license."

"Weird. How did he explain that?"

"He had no idea how it happened—at least that's what he says."

"How did you end up hiring a male electrician? Is he from Island Electric?"

"No. Island Electric went out of business and I'm trying not to subcontract these days—cuts too much into my profits. Besides, Leslie is also a carpenter. He does pretty much everything."

"How did you find this gem?"

"I didn't," Josie answered, and then explained how Nic had found the crew for her.

"Sounds like you were surprised when a man showed up on the job."

"Yes, but you know Island Contracting has no policy against hiring men. And Vicki, Leslie's fiancée, is working for me this summer as well."

"So how long has Leslie been missing his identification?"

"He says he lost his license awhile ago, and when he realized it, he applied for a replacement. He's been carrying the replacement ever since then. He claims to have no idea how his original license ended up on the body. In fact, he claims to have lost his license more than once and didn't even know it."

"Isn't that odd? How could you lose your driver's license?"

Josie considered. "You know me. I'm always losing things. My driver's license could vanish and I might not realize it—not unless I was stopped by the police and asked to produce it."

Betty grinned. "If you were stopped on the island, the Rodneys wouldn't bother to ask for your license. They know who you are."

"Only too well," Josie agreed.

Gert reappeared, a big smile on her face. "So, which one will it be?"

"Which what?" Josie began before realizing what she was being asked. "Oh, the dress. Can you give me a few days to think about it?"

"You're being married on Labor Day?"

"Yes."

"I can give you two weeks. I can put a rush on any gown you pick as a favor to dear Carol, but it will still take a month to make it."

"That's great!"

"But two weeks is the absolute limit, my dear. You be sure to come back in before then."

"I . . . do I need to come back in?"

"Of course you do. For your fitting."

"You can't do it long distance? I run a business on the shore. I don't know if I can get away again."

Gert pursed her lips. "I don't see how . . ."

"What if you measure Josie right now?" Betty asked.

"I can do that, of course, but each dress is completely individual. Once you pick out your gown, there will still be questions. Of course, if you decide now . . ."

Josie hadn't run her own business for years without learning that there were times when her only option was to make a quick decision and stick with it. "The sheath with the bolero," she said.

Betty jumped up and hugged her friend. "Oh, you're going to have a formal wedding!"

"And it's a decision you'll never regret, my dear. Now take off your clothes. Let's get busy and get those measurements."

Josie stripped down to her bra and underpants. Gert was wrong—she already regretted her decision.

One of the many mistakes the Rodneys had made was to arrest Betty for murder years before. That mistake had led to her meeting and, in time, marrying Jon Jacobs. Jon and Sam, both attorneys, had known each other in New York City, where they had been on the opposite sides of many cases when Sam worked as a city prosecutor and Jon was a lawyer hired by the defense. Even now, years after Sam's move to the island, they spoke on the phone regularly. But Jon had become something of a wine expert and their conversations these days, as far as Josie could tell, were frequently more about wine than law. Now, sitting in Betty's beautifully decorated living room in her prewar co-op, Josie was trying to figure out how to convince Jon to help her without talking to Sam about it.

They had demolished a feast of Thai food before Betty and Jon had disappeared to put JJ to bed. So far their talk had been about the baby and the wedding. Now

Jon, his shirtfront a bit damp from helping with his son's bath, reappeared and sat down across from his guest. "More wine?" he asked, picking up the bottle of Riesling they had enjoyed with dinner.

"I think I'm fine, thanks. Does Betty need any help with JJ?"

"No. The truth is, she's better off putting him to sleep by herself. JJ hates to sleep when he thinks something else is going on. We turn off all the lights and close the curtains—sort of bore him to sleep," Jon explained, pouring the last of the wine into his glass and sipping. "This actually goes very well with the spiciness of Thai food, don't you think?"

She knew nothing about wine, but she was used to agreeing with the experts. "Excellent. How are things going at work?"

"Oh, you know. Same old, same old. How's Island Contracting? Betty says you have another murder on your hands."

"Oh, I don't think the body has anything to do with us," Josie answered. "But I do have a problem that you might be able to help me with . . ."

"Anything. You know that, Josie. But if it's a legal problem, why not ask Sam?"

Josie took a deep breath and repeated the lie she had come up with during dinner. "It's not exactly a legal problem. See, I'm trying to make sure everything—absolutely everything—having to do with Island Contracting is organized and on my computer before the wedding." She paused. "You know how organized Sam is . . ."

"And you're not?" Jon guessed.

Josie was fairly sure that Sam had complained about

this very thing to Jon, probably more than once, so she thought he wouldn't question her next words. "Not at all, and things have gotten into a terrible mess. To tell you the truth, I don't want Sam to realize how messy everything is."

Jon nodded. "So how can I help you?"

Josie had just finished explaining what she needed when Betty returned to the room. They opened another bottle of wine and were still talking when JJ woke up at two A.M.

TWENTY-TWO

JOSIE WAS TIRED and just a bit hungover on her drive back to the island. But she had accomplished more in her short time in the city than she would have thought possible in her most optimistic moment.

The connection between Betty and Maud Higgins might or might not reveal something useful. Betty had promised to talk to Maud about her grandparents right away. "Probably today," she had added, waving JJ's hand in the air as Josie started her truck and pulled out into the speeding traffic. Driving in New York City was as different from driving at home as it was possible to get. Josie had panicked until Sam pointed out that each driver was responsible only for his own front fender. It didn't make a lot of sense, but it always worked, and Josie made it to the Garden State Parkway without incident.

Once out of the city, traffic was light and Josie allowed herself to think of something other than the road. She reviewed her conversation with Jon. After admitting she was sometimes unsure how long she had to keep legal documents pertaining to her business—and relating an incident concerning the Internal Revenue Service and a lost contract—she had mentioned health insurance. With crews changing from year to year, and sometimes from month to month, Josie had a fair number of insignificant questions she could ask without exposing the dire situation she found her company in.

It was Jon who brought up what happened to companies when they were denied health insurance. He had worked on a case the year before—some sort of lawsuit that his firm had handled—where an uninsured employee had sued his employer for medical costs and damages when he was taken ill and needed surgery, two months of hospitalization, and a year of physical therapy. Josie didn't remember all the details, but she did remember Jon's point: you can't sign away your rights. What this meant to Josie and Island Contracting was that even if she asked Leslie to put in writing his acceptance of working uninsured, he would still be able to sue at a later date. It had not been encouraging.

But his most interesting statement had been something like, "Of course, it might have been different if the company hadn't been able to get insurance—in this instance, their insurance carrier had raised their premiums, and the company had refused to pay them. You see, the responsibility had landed right in the employer's lap."

Josie realized a few things at that moment: that Leslie's situation was unique and didn't have anything to do with the rest of her crew, that she was glad she had decided to pay the higher premiums regardless of the increased cost, and that her decision to keep this bit of information from Sam had been a good one. Sam was personally and professionally cautious and would insist that she fire Leslie.

So she would spend the summer lying to the man she

loved while planning a large formal wedding that she didn't want as she remodeled a house with an uninsured worker—and for minimal profit if she decided to replenish her nest egg. And that was ignoring the murder. Praying the police wouldn't have set up a speed trap this early, she slammed the accelerator to the floor. Time to get on with her life.

Unfortunately, there was a speed trap and Josie got on with her life over an hour later than she had planned. But her late arrival didn't explain the frown on Mary Ann's face or the tears on Vicki's cheeks. Leslie's arrest did.

Vicki was crying too hard to speak coherently, but Mary Ann explained that the police had arrived with a warrant for Leslie's arrest a few hours before. Nic had gone to the police station to find out what, if anything, could be done to release him.

"I wanted to go, but they thought Nic would be better," Vicki sobbed.

Josie agreed with that. "Did either of the Rodneys explain why he was being arrested? Do they have any new information connecting Leslie to the dead man?"

"We don't know. The three of them appeared soon after we all got here this morning."

"The three of them? Trish Petric was here too?"

"Yeah."

"They put handcuffs on him and led him out the door like a common criminal," Vicki said.

"We tried to keep working after Leslie left, but . . ." Mary Ann shrugged and looked over at Vicki.

Josie frowned. "I guess I should go down to the station."

"Oh no, please, please don't do that!" Vicki cried.

"Why not?"

"The younger officer . . ."

"Mike Rodney?" Josie asked.

"Yes, I guess. He said for you to keep out of their investigation if you knew what was good for you—and for Leslie."

"I told her that you didn't have to listen to anything like that," Mary Ann said to Josie.

"But you're not going to go there, are you? Please don't!"

"No, I'll stay here—but we have to get some work done," Josie ended firmly.

"The windows for the top floor were delivered yesterday afternoon while you were in the city," Mary Ann said. "We were planning to start replacing the old ones today and surprise you when you returned. I guess that's out now, but they're the smallest windows in the house—the three of us can manage easily."

"Maybe Vicki doesn't feel up to working . . ." Josie began.

"I can help. It will keep me from thinking about the atrocities that might be happening to Leslie in jail," Vicki said.

Josie smiled. "I don't think you have to worry about anything happening to Leslie. The only jail on the island is a holding cell at the back of the police station. I understand the worst the prisoners suffer is having to choose between pizza from Island Pies and seafood from Sylvester's take-out for dinner."

"Oh. Leslie loves Sylvester's fried scallops." Vicki perked up. "Do you think I'll be able to visit him?"

"Of course you will," Mary Ann said. "Perhaps they'll even allow conjugal visits," she added sarcastically.

Vicki took a deep breath and dried her eyes on her sleeve. "I guess I can work now."

Josie breathed a sigh of relief. "Let's get going."

They worked hard for four hours, pausing to order pizza from Island Pies. Vicki questioned the delivery man and discovered that he had made a delivery to the police station just a few hours before. "Pepperoni and peppers—Leslie's favorite," she reported to Josie and Mary Ann. They were just installing the last window on the front facade when Sam appeared.

"So you've decided on a formal affair," he said, smiling and kissing the top of Josie's head as he brushed sawdust off his pant legs.

For a moment, she was completely mystified before remembering the dress being altered for her back in New York City at this very moment. "Gert called Carol, right?"

"Right! Mom's thrilled. But we have lots of things to do. I thought we should start with dinner tonight at Basil's. That's the logical place for the reception, don't you think?"

"But I thought Risa . . . Oh damn, Sam, I can't think about that right now."

"Josie, you've made the important decision. Now all we have to do is figure out where to hold the reception after the wedding."

"Sam, Leslie was arrested for the murder of that man."

"What man?"

"The body found here."

Sam changed gears with apparent ease. "They've identified him?"

"I don't know. I was in the city . . . well, actually I was driving home when he was arrested. I don't think anyone said anything about the identity of the victim. Did they?" she turned to Vicki and Mary Ann, who were busy nailing the bead board to the wall beneath one of the new windows.

"No."

"I don't remember them saying anything about who he is."

"Really? That's odd."

"Why, Sam?"

"Usually a warrant is issued for the arrest of someone for murder. Like you see on TV: 'You're under arrest for the murder of John Doe.' Although, of course, it's never exactly like it is on television."

"It certainly wasn't like that here," Mary Ann said.

"Why not? What did they say?" Josie asked.

"Yes, what happened, exactly?" Sam added.

"Well, we were all sitting around eating doughnuts," Mary Ann began. She looked over at Josie and continued. "I know it sounds bad, but we all worked late last night—it was almost nine when I finally got home—and so we had agreed to meet here at eight."

"Except for Leslie," Vicki pointed out. "He just dropped me off and then went to the bakery to pick up breakfast for us. It only took a few extra minutes. And we had worked . . ."

"Late last night. That's fine," Josie assured her. "You all did a lot while I was gone. I have nothing to complain about. Go on with your story."

"Well, it's not that I'm trying to defend Leslie—or

us—but he really got back here in record time. Anyway, we all settled down to eat," Mary Ann continued.

"Where?"

"We were sitting in the front parlor. It's so gorgeous outside today and the sun comes in through the big bay window."

Josie realized that they had chosen to sit there because they would be able to see her if she drove up, and she wouldn't be able to see whether or not they were working if she did appear. But she had faith in these women; the work they had done the day before proved their worth. And she knew that sometimes it was important to give everyone some slack. "Were you in a position to see the Rodneys and Trish Petric arrive?"

"Yes, and you wouldn't have believed it—they drove up in two cruisers."

"Two-thirds of the island's police fleet, in fact," Sam pointed out.

"Yes. And their lights were flashing."

"They used their sirens?" Josie asked Mary Ann.

"No, just the lights," she answered.

"But they left the lights flashing at the curb when they got out and came to the door," Vicki added to Mary Ann's description.

"That's right. They left the lights flashing and came in and announced that they had come to arrest Leslie."

Sam asked a question. "Who spoke?"

"The son of the police chief. He introduced himself as Officer Michael Rodney and said that Officer Petric and his father, the chief of the island's police force, were here to arrest Leslie Coyne and that they hoped there wouldn't be any trouble. They actually had their hands on the guns in their holsters!"

"Well, if Leslie were a killer—and that's what they're claiming, not what I'm saying—he very well might have been armed . . ."

"And dangerous," Vicki finished Sam's statement. "But Leslie wasn't—isn't like that! He's sweet and kind and would never kill anyone for anything. Never! You have to believe me!"

"We believe you," Josie said.

"But it doesn't matter what we believe," Sam pointed out. "What matters is what the police think, and what they know that we don't know."

"They don't know anything really important! They don't know Leslie!" Vicki cried.

"I know that's how you're feeling, but they arrested him, yes? So they must have connected him to the dead man—whose name you're sure they didn't mention?" Sam's voice remained calm, but Josie suspected he was finding this conversation more than a little trying.

"I'm sure they didn't mention it," Mary Ann said. "In fact, they didn't say anything about murder. Or Leslie's identification being found on the body or anything like that. They just said they were going to arrest him. Period."

"Yeah. Can you believe any police force in the world would make such a big deal over a few too many speeding tickets?" Leslie appeared in the doorway.

"Les!" Vicki was at his side and in his arms in an instant.

Nic stood behind Leslie, beaming. In fact, Josie realized, everyone in the room was smiling except for Sam. And Sam, it seemed, had a few questions.

"So you were arrested for speeding?" he asked.

"Yeah, can you believe that? They saw me speeding

on my way back from the bakery this morning, they looked up my name on their computers and saw that I had points on my license for other tickets, and they just hauled me in for questioning."

"In fact, I can believe that." Sam still wasn't smiling. "And I'd sure like to know what questions they asked."

TWENTY-THREE

THE TONE OF the room changed immediately as everyone realized the implications of Sam's question.

Vicki, still in Leslie's arms, looked up at him. "What did they ask you? What did you tell them? Were you careful?"

"Careful? What did I have to be careful about? They had a complete record of my tickets . . . there wasn't much there that I could have lied about."

"But the murder . . . did they ask you about the murder?" Mary Ann asked.

"They asked me about my tickets. The young cop—Mike something—damn near drove me nuts asking me over and over about the tickets."

"You said they had a complete record of your moving violations," Sam pointed out. "What was there to ask you about?"

"That's what you would have thought, and you would have been wrong," Leslie said. "He asked where I was picked up and when I was picked up and if I had to appear in court, and then what sort of fine I paid. He asked where I was living when I got each ticket, how long I had been living there . . ." He glanced over at Vicki before continuing. "... who I was living with, where I was working. It took a long time, I can tell you."

"Just how many tickets have you gotten?" Sam asked the question that Josie was curious about.

"Nine."

"But you're not old enough to get that many tickets," Josie exclaimed.

"I'm twenty-nine. Been driving since I was sixteen—that's thirteen years," Leslie added as though he was the only one in the group capable of solving this equation.

"How many times have you talked a police officer out of giving you a ticket?" Sam asked.

"Hey, man, I'm not sure I can count that high!" Leslie beamed, and Josie realized he thought he was being clever.

"Well, I guess all those tickets are the reason the island police had so many questions for you," Josie said.

"Maybe." Sam sounded as though he didn't agree with her assessment of the situation. "As I understand it, they asked where you got the tickets, where you were living when you got them, who you were living with, and where you were working."

"Yeah."

"Were you driving your own vehicles each time you were picked up?"

"Nah. Sometimes I was driving a car—or truck, probably—that belonged to the company I was working for, and sometimes the car belonged to someone I knew."

"A friend?" Sam asked.

"Yeah, a friend."

"Like when you were stopped last week, you were driving my car," Vicki pointed out.

"This was your second ticket since you started working here?" Josie asked, a bit incredulous.

"Nope. I was picked up by the babe—by the woman police officer—and she didn't give me a ticket."

"You mean you charmed your way out of a ticket," Sam suggested.

"Les can charm his way out of anything," Vicki said. It didn't sound to Josie as though she was bragging.

"I guess she thought I was cute." Leslie had the grace to sound as though the fact embarrassed him—a little.

"Other than that time, have the island police given you any tickets?" Sam asked.

"Nope. I've gotten pretty good at making sure I see the cops before they see me," Leslie explained. "Took me a few days before I realized they were always hanging out in that delivery area behind Hoy's five-and-ten, but now that I've got that scoped out, I think we can be sure they won't be picking me up again."

"You could just drive under the speed limit," Sam suggested.

"You *should* drive under the speed limit," Josie said. "The island is full of tourists these days and there are lots of kids on bikes and skateboards. They're having fun and they won't be paying much attention to safety. You have to look out for them and that means staying under twenty-five miles an hour." Josie knew she was lecturing, and she knew she didn't always practice what she was preaching, but years of motherhood got the better of her.

"Yeah, I'll be more careful," Leslie said. "Really," he added. "To tell the truth, it was a little creepy being taken down to the police station like that."

"Why couldn't they just question you here?" Vicki asked. "Why do they keep taking you away?"

"And why the handcuffs?" Mary Ann asked.

"They handcuffed you?" Sam asked.

"Yeah. You see," Leslie began, hesitating for the first time. "You see, I had sort of left town—well, two towns— before paying my fines. Apparently they thought that was more serious than I did. I mean, they were just speeding tickets," he reminded them.

"What do you think, Sam?" Josie asked.

"It's possible that those tickets, whether paid or not, were just an excuse to question him," Sam answered.

"So you think there's something significant about those questions, right?"

"I can't think of any other explanation."

Josie turned to Leslie. "And they only asked you about where you worked and lived when you got those nine tickets, right?"

"Yeah."

"So that must be it—there must be something significant about one of those places, maybe something that relates to the murdered man," Josie continued.

"I don't see the connection . . ." Sam began, but Leslie interrupted him.

"Yeah. They were talking about the murder in the police car," Leslie spoke up.

"About you in relation to the murder?" Josie asked.

"They think you're the killer?" Vicki said, starting to cry again.

"Nah, they weren't thinking about me. They were thinking about Josie."

"What about me?" Josie asked, her voice rising at least an octave.

"What did they say about Josie?" Sam asked more calmly. "Exactly."

"The younger officer—he's the chief's son, right?"

"Yes, he is. Just one of the many idiosyncrasies of the force here on the island. Go on," Sam answered.

"He mentioned the murder first. He said something about Josie and Island Contracting being involved in a murder investigation again."

"What do you mean, something about it?" Sam asked.

"I don't remember exactly. I was trying to get comfortable—it's not easy when your hands are cuffed together behind your back, let me tell you."

"I can imagine," Sam said patiently. "But you do remember that he mentioned Josie and Island Contracting, right?"

"Yeah. Both Josie and the company. I'm sure of that."

Sam asked another question. "And what did his father say?"

"His father? Oh, his father wasn't in the car with us. He led the way in his car. The woman officer was driving."

"Really?"

"Do you think that's significant, Sam?" Josie asked.

"I haven't the foggiest. So Trish Petric was driving and Mike Rodney was riding shotgun and Mike brought up murder and Josie, just like that."

"Yeah. Made me nervous as hell, too. I thought they were going to arrest me for killing that guy we found. I told them that I didn't have anything to do with the guy—didn't even know him. Just because they found my driver's license doesn't mean a thing. But they ignored me. They just kept talking about murders on the island and how someone from Island Contracting always turned out to be involved. And then we got to the station and Chief Rodney had them take me into his office, and he started asking me about my speeding tickets. That's all."

"Are you telling us that no one mentioned the murders or Josie or Island Contracting after you got to the police station?" Sam asked.

"Yup. They were just interested in my tickets once we got there."

"Didn't you think that was strange?" Mary Ann asked.

"Hell, I was just relieved that they weren't going to arrest me. If they wanted to waste their time talking about a bunch of old tickets, who was I to complain?"

Josie looked at Sam. "What do you think?"

He shrugged. "Who knows what goes on in the minds of the island police? You know how it is."

She did and she didn't. But one thing she was sure of: They were wasting time. "Then we better get back to work. Those windows aren't going to put themselves in." She stood up and stretched her arms high above her head. "I'll see you tonight, Sam?"

"I'll pick you up at home."

"How about at my office? I need to feed the kittens," Josie suggested. "Around seven?"

"Sounds good to me."

"You guys get to work and I'll walk Sam to his car," Josie ordered.

She was the boss, they were her crew. In less than five minutes she and Sam were alone. "What do you really think?" she demanded, after a series of loud thumps convinced her that work was being done.

"That something fishy is going on here. The Rodneys are idiots, but they're not complete idiots. They must have taken Leslie down to the station for a reason."

"But what?" she asked.

"Damned if I know. Just how much do you know about Leslie Coyne?"

"Not much. He has some sort of health condition, but it doesn't affect his work," she added, realizing she was steering too close to a topic she didn't want to introduce. "He's an excellent electrician."

"Women like him. You like him," Sam interrupted.

She looked up at him. "Don't tell me you're jealous."

"He's young. He's good-looking. He spends most of each day with you." Sam looked down at Josie. "I am a bit jealous. I don't think I'd ever appreciated your dedication to hiring women who need to change their lives until Leslie appeared on the scene."

Josie smiled. "I don't think anyone has ever been jealous of another man because of me before."

"Get used to it. I'm planning on being jealous of all the men in your life forever. Now, back to the subject at hand . . ."

"Why the Rodneys took Leslie down to the station and asked him about his past tickets," Josie said.

"Yes."

"Do you think it had something to do with his past? The jobs he had? The places he lived? The women he was involved with? That's what they asked him about, right?"

"Right. And that's the problem. The only way we're

going to know what they really were investigating is to look at all those things and figure out what might interest the police."

"Like what?"

"Like did he date someone involved in criminal activities? Was he involved in something criminal in one of the places or on one of the jobs in his past? I think we can assume that the Rodneys knew what they were looking for."

"But we don't, do we?"

"Not unless Leslie has been more honest with you than I think he has," Sam said.

Josie thought about that for a moment. "He hasn't said anything to me, but maybe Vicki knows more about him than I do, and maybe I can get her to tell me what it is."

"Sounds like a good idea to me." Sam frowned. "How do you know Leslie has a health problem?"

"Oh, you know, insurance forms," Josie said, keeping her answer purposely vague.

Sam frowned, but he didn't say anything more on the subject. "You said you want me to pick you up at the office?"

"Yes. We're going to be working late and I want to check my answering machine before we go out tonight. Besides, I need to feed the kittens."

Sam kissed her on the top of her head. "Only you would try to run a kitten adoption agency out of your office. Are you expecting an important call?"

"Backorders at the hardware store. You know how it is," Josie lied.

"Just as long as they don't take too long. I promised Basil we'd meet him at seven-thirty. We have a lot of decisions to make if we're going to ask Basil to cater our reception."

Josie tried to smile. She had a few decisions to make herself, and none of them had to do with their wedding. They were things she would rather keep to herself.

TWENTY-FOUR

I F FIVE PEOPLE are working to replace a small window, at least two of them are going to be in the way, so Josie was able to maneuver some time alone with Vicki—who, she discovered, was anxious to talk with her.

"Do you think the police are going to arrest Leslie?" Vicki asked as the two women began to rip layers of cracked and filthy linoleum off the floor of one of the third floor half-baths.

Josie put down her crowbar and sat back on her work boots, determined to be the one to ask questions. "Not unless he's guilty of something other than not paying speeding tickets. And he isn't, is he?"

Vicki's crow bar crashed to the floor. "Of course he isn't! You don't know Leslie the way I do! He's kind and sweet and nice and good and . . ."

"And honest?" Josie asked when Vicki's list of Leslie's virtues dwindled off.

"Of course he's honest! He's always been honest with me. In fact, he even told me that he was involved with someone else when we met. Not many men do that, do they?"

"I haven't been involved with all that many men,"

Josie admitted. "But, to tell the truth, I don't think I'd want a man I was involved with to be involved with someone else—and telling me about it wouldn't make it better. At least I don't think it would. If you understand what I mean."

"But it's not like that. I love Leslie. I loved him the very moment I saw him. I didn't care about the other woman when he told me about her. It was all over—or it was about to end—when we met, and I loved him immediately."

Josie realized she wasn't going to learn anything if Vicki thought she was being judgmental. "Of course. And it's obvious that he cares deeply about you," she said hesitantly. She actually had no idea how Leslie felt about Vicki, and he seemed to flirt with every woman he came in contact with. "How did you meet?" she asked.

"At the convention in Washington. I thought Nic would have told you that."

"You met in DC? Right before you came here?"

"It was love at first sight," Vicki explained earnestly.

"For both of you? I mean, how do you know what Leslie was feeling?"

"He told me that it was the same for him," Vicki answered proudly. "He said he had never felt the way he felt about me before—you know, instantly in love."

"Yeah, I think that's probably sort of rare for anyone." Josie was afraid she might sound a bit sarcastic.

If so, Vicki didn't appear to realize it. "Oh, it is!" she gushed. "Our meeting was so lucky. I was going to come here alone. I'd already rented my apartment and everything. And Leslie was going to take a job somewhere in the South. If we hadn't met when we did and fallen in love immediately, why, we could be living hundreds of miles apart. We might never, ever have run into each other."

"So you two are living in an apartment you rented before you met Leslie," Josie commented.

"Yes. Wasn't that lucky? We came here when everyone else did, but we had a few days to drive around, walk on the beach, get to know the place. Leslie says he doesn't really feel comfortable until he's spent some time wandering around alone."

"And you're paying for the apartment?"

"I know how it sounds, but I don't mind paying the rent myself—I was planning to anyway. And I know Leslie will pay me back when he gets on his feet again. That girl he was involved with when he met me sounds like a real witch—or a real bitch to tell the truth."

"Why do you say that? What did she do?"

"She took everything he had. It was just awful!"

Josie repeated her last question. "But what did she do?"

Vicki ripped up a long chunk of linoleum before answering.

"She lied about being pregnant."

"Leslie left a woman who was pregnant?"

"No! He would never do that. She told him she was pregnant and that she needed money for an abortion. Leslie was shocked—she had told him that she was taking birth control pills. And he offered to do the right thing and marry her. He didn't love her at all, so it was really wonderful of him to offer, don't you think?"

Josie was relieved that Vicki didn't stop talking long enough to listen to what she thought.

"She insisted that he give her money for an abortion and then she didn't have one."

Josie's own history didn't allow her to ignore this one. "He left her pregnant?" she asked again.

"No! That's just the point. She wasn't pregnant. She just wanted the money. And you wouldn't believe what she used the money he gave her for."

"No, probably not."

"Tattoos! She wanted to get tattoos! Do you believe that? Doesn't she sound just awful?"

"She certainly doesn't sound like a very nice person. Why do you think Leslie stayed with her?"

For the first time in the conversation, Vicki seemed uncertain of her answer. "I think that maybe he felt sorry for her. He did say that she was a pathological liar—almost unable to distinguish between the truth and fiction."

Josie was busy trying to wedge her paint scraper beneath a particularly well-glued section of flooring, so she didn't reply for a minute.

"It's not that I haven't wondered if maybe Leslie was taking advantage of her—living in her home and all—but he told me that he felt he had to take care of her, that she shouldn't be living alone. He thought it might not be safe for her to be on her own, considering her psychological problems."

"But when he met you?"

"He fell in love and knew he had to be with me. And he decided he shouldn't sacrifice his life for that other girl. He saw someone on television—one of those shows that has a therapist helping people—and that man, a real qualified doctor, said it wasn't healthy to give up your dreams for another person. So he came here to the island with me."

"It's lucky you two met each other when you did,"

Josie said, meaning—but not saying—that it had certainly been lucky for Leslie.

"Oh, it is. I don't know what I would have done if I hadn't met him. I'm so happy now!"

"I just hope the island police don't do something stupid," Josie said.

"They can't really believe that Leslie would do anything illegal . . ."

"Other than speeding and not paying his tickets."

"Yes, but that's not the same as murder!"

"No, of course not." Josie paused before continuing. "Do you have any idea why the police are so interested in Leslie's past? Where he worked and lived and all that?"

"I trust Leslie."

"Yes, of course. I can't imagine being romantically involved with anyone I didn't trust, but the truth is I don't know everything that happened in Sam's past."

"No, I don't know much about Leslie's past either," Vicki admitted. "But I haven't known Leslie as long as you've known Sam."

"Were you surprised by Leslie's driving record? All those speeding tickets." Josie turned away and worked with her back to Vicki.

"Yeah, I was. You don't think it affects my driving record in any way, do you? My parents gave me my car when I graduated from the local community college and they still pay my insurance. I sure wouldn't want them to have to pay higher premiums."

"Is it your car that Leslie is driving?"

"Yes. His car . . . well, I'm not exactly sure what happened to it, but I think the woman he was involved with has it for some reason or other."

"So . . ." Josie began slowly.

"I know what you're thinking. You're thinking that Leslie is taking advantage of me. But it's not true. He loves me. It just doesn't always look like that . . . I mean, I don't want people to misunderstand."

"I don't doubt that he loves you," Josie lied. "But I know better than almost anyone else on the island how incompetent the Rodneys and the police department are. And I don't understand why Leslie was hauled down to the police department and asked all those questions. And I do need to know—not because I distrust Leslie, but because I need to protect my company and this job. We can't do this job without Leslie, and believe me, the Rodneys can make things very difficult for all of us if they decide to."

"You think that Leslie was questioned for a reason. I mean, you think the police know something about him that might involve some sort of illegal activity. Right?"

"It's possible, isn't it?"

"Leslie would never break the law, except for speeding."

"But what if someone he knows—or knew—did something illegal and the police are interested in that? Leslie might not even know about it. But he might have told you about that person or something happening that seemed unusual at the time . . . or something like that."

Vicki put down her tools, wiped sweat off her forehead, and straightened her shoulders. "Leslie is always involved with a woman. No matter where he lives or where he works, he always has a girlfriend. That I do know. I don't know who all of them are, of course. I mean, we've talked about our past—like you do—but sometimes he leaves out details, like where he was living when he was dating the woman who worked as an exotic dancer. Maybe Vegas? I know he worked there for a while. Or even when he dated the women. I get confused, but I would remember if he had told me about anything illegal. He didn't even mention those tickets." She smiled. "He probably wanted to protect me."

"That doesn't surprise me too much," Josie said, although she was convinced that the only person Leslie was really interested in protecting was himself.

TWENTY-FIVE

THE CREW WORKED hard, and by six-thirty everyone was tired and hungry. Nic was getting into her purple truck when Josie caught up with her outside of the Bride's Secret Bed and Breakfast. "Do you have a few minutes?" she asked.

"Sure. Do you need a ride somewhere?"

"Ah . . . yeah, could you take me to my office?"

"Sure. What about your truck?"

Josie looked over her shoulder at Island Contracting's red truck waiting by the curb. "Not running," she answered. "Guess I'll have to splurge on a new battery."

"Want a jump?" Nic nodded to the jumper cables tangled on the floor behind the driver's seat.

"No. Thanks though. Sam's meeting me at the office. He'll drive me back here and we'll take care of the truck. He's probably there already."

"Okay. Let's go. Don't want to keep your man waiting." Nic switched on the ignition, put her truck in gear, and pulled away from the curb.

"Actually," Josie began, "I wanted to talk to you, but I didn't want anyone else on the crew to know."

"Gonna give me a raise and you don't want them to be jealous, huh?"

"I wish I could give you all a raise. We're right on schedule despite all the problems."

"If you call finding a body a problem, you really are used to murder. Like everyone says."

"Sounds sort of callous, doesn't it?"

"A bit," Nic admitted. "So what do you want to talk to me about? Leslie and Vicki?"

"Good guess."

"I'm no Sherlock Holmes. It's just that Leslie was hauled in by the police this morning, and then you spent the afternoon working alone with Vicki out of hearing of the rest of us. You could have worked in the bathroom next door to where we were doing windows instead of all the way down the hallway if you hadn't wanted some privacy."

"I had a few questions for her," Josie admitted.

"And now you have some for me."

"Yeah. I was wondering how you met the two of them. It was at the convention, right?"

"Right. I met Vicki first. She was having a drink in the bar of the convention hotel with an old friend of mine, a woman I worked with up north on a few jobs. Anyway, I had been talking the night before about hiring carpenters for this job, and Vicki needed work, so we talked for a bit. She had come to the con to find a job and had her resumé in order. I looked it over and thought she had some good experience and references. My friend said they had worked together, so I suggested she come here and meet you."

"She said she had rented an apartment before coming here."

"Really? Listen, I didn't promise her a job. I made it

clear to her—and to Mary Ann and Leslie—that you're the boss and do the hiring."

"I'm not accusing you of anything. You found me a great crew and every one of them knew that I was doing the hiring. It's just . . . I'm interested in the apartment because I found myself wondering if Leslie's romantic interest in Vicki was inspired by the fact that she had an apartment and a car."

"Yeah, I thought that too."

"You don't like Leslie?"

"Look, my life was damn near ruined by a man. Let's just say I'm always suspicious of men who are supported by women."

"She's supporting him?"

"Well, he buys pizza sometimes and picks up the tab at the bakery in the morning, but I think that might be it. I know when I run into Vic at the grocery store, she's there alone, and she's paying with the money she's earned, I'll bet."

"How did you meet Leslie?"

"Vicki told me about him the night before I left D.C., but I didn't actually meet him until the next day. I was dumping my bag into the back of my truck, and she came up to me in the parking lot and introduced us. I was surprised Leslie was a man, but being a licensed electrician, I thought you'd be interested. We'd had such problems getting electricians all winter."

"Yeah, there was no way I was going to turn down a competent electrician," Josie agreed. "But did you know they were going to be living together when you told Leslie about Island Contracting?"

"Nope. I knew Vicki had a humongous crush on him, though—anyone looking at the two of them could tell that. My granny used to talk about people in love having stars in their eyes, and Vicki had the whole Milky Way in hers."

"And Leslie?"

"Look, I don't want to trash Leslie. As far as I know he's a good guy: works well with women, treats us all like equals, doesn't make a lot of sexist jokes. But at the same time he does think he's god's gift to women, and he takes Vicki's adoration the same way he takes her money—for granted. And that's what was going on when I met him. She had those stars in her eyes and he was preening. Anyone could have seen that they'd spent the night together, but no one said it went beyond that. I did think for a second or two that a lone man on an all-female crew might be a potential problem, but, hell, we're all adults . . ."

"Yeah, you're right." They had arrived at the office and Josie opened the passenger's seat door and prepared to hop down. "Thanks for the ride."

"No problem. Give me a yell if you think of any more questions. I'll be hanging out in my apartment all evening."

Josie smiled. "See you tomorrow. Bright and early."

"You got it!"

Josie might have said more if she hadn't realized that her son was waiting for her, lounging on the small porch that connected her office with the street. "Tyler!"

"Hi, Mom."

"What are you doing here?"

"Waiting for you. And I fed the kittens . . . I may even have found a home for one."

"That's great. Then I won't go inside. Sam is meeting me here."

"Oh, I thought maybe we could talk."

"What's wrong?"

"Why do you always think there's something wrong?"

"I don't always think any such thing," Josie replied honestly. Tyler was a good kid and had never given her any real problems. "It's just that we haven't spent much time together since you came home for vacation. Sam and I are going to one of Basil's places for dinner—why don't you come along? You can have some of those mussels you like so much."

"I already ate. I had mussels, too. Risa was trying a new recipe—she's always trying new recipes these days. Have you noticed? It's not like her, is it?"

"Maybe she's decided it's time to try something new," Josie commented. She wasn't much interested. All of her landlady's meals were wonderful, whether she was using family recipes from her childhood in Italy or something she had seen the night before on the Food Network.

"Yeah, maybe. These were wonderful. I think I'm beginning to gain weight." He pulled his jeans away from his slender waist and frowned.

"You look just fine. Listen, Tyler, I can't stand up Sam, but if you're still awake when I get home . . ."

"I've got a late date, Mom. Movie on the pier—a bunch of us are going to the show and then out for pizza or something. It may be late before I'm in."

"How about breakfast at Sullivan's tomorrow morning?"

"Yeah, okay. Nine o'clock?"

"More like seven. I have to be at the Bride's Secret by seven-thirty. Can't expect my crew to work without me."

"Well . . . maybe. If I'm up that early." They both knew he wouldn't be, and Josie was about to suggest an alternative meal when Tyler changed the subject. "You know, at work we're making up brochures for the supermarket, and I was talking to one of the old guys there. He said his father used to tell stories about the bride disappearing on the night before her wedding and . . . hey, there's Sam's MGB. Guess I'd better split if you two are going to dinner."

"Tyler . . ." But her son had hopped on his bike and was off, speeding down the street, pausing only to wave at his mother and her fiancé.

"Where's he off to?" Sam asked, waving back.

"The movies and pizza."

"I hope the island police don't see him—I think he rides that bike over the speed limit."

"But the speed limit doesn't apply to bicycles, does it?"

"I don't think so. And I was just kidding. So, shall we head over to Basil's?"

"My truck is at the Bride's Secret, but we can pick it up after dinner. I'm starving."

"Why did you leave your truck there?"

"I wanted to talk to Nic, and it was easiest to do that on the way here, so I rode along with her."

Sam didn't have any more questions, and they rode over to Basil's in his MGB, top down, the warm evening wind in their hair. "I think I'd better visit the lady's room before anyone sees me," Josie said, getting out of the car and patting down her red mop, making absolutely no improvement in her appearance.

"Basil is meeting us in the bar."

"I'll be there in a few minutes," she answered.

Basil's place had the best food on the island, but the ambience was casual. Although Josie's overalls weren't in the same price range as the average tourist's Brooks Brothers polo shirts, chinos, and boat shoes, she didn't look too terribly out of place—once she had spent some time washing her face and hands and tying a bandanna over her hair. As promised, Sam and Basil were in the bar, sitting before a table covered with an array of pastel cocktails.

"Wow! What is all this?"

Basil, whom no one had ever seen wearing anything by Brooks Brothers, jumped up from his seat, his sharkskin slacks, red silk shirt, and a Hermes tie wound through his belt loops, causing him to stand out in the crowd. "Champagne, of course. Vintage if Sam's store carries such, but I thought imaginative cocktails as well. Apple of My Eye Martini. Wedded Bliss Rum Punch. Connubial Cosmopolitan. Marriage Mimosa. Vows Vodka Shots."

Basil pointed from glass to glass as he listed the drinks. "We can, of course, serve all of them, but I thought you might just pick two or three."

There were at least a dozen drinks on the table. "You want us to taste them all?" Josie asked, reaching for a large goblet of pale orange liquid.

"Just a sip," Sam said as she gulped down more than half the contents of the glass.

"Wow! That's fantastic! What's in it?"

"Champagne, Grand Marnier, orange juice, and cherry brandy. It's a variation on the classic mimosa."

"It's delicious," Josie said, finishing off her drink.

"Maybe we should eat as we drink."

"I'm starving," Josie pointed out, as she felt the warmth of the alcohol begin to ward off the room's chilly air conditioning.

"We'll need to discuss main courses at a later date. I've only laid out my favorite appetizers and first courses, but I think we can make a meal of them." Basil pointed to a table laden with dozens of tiny plates and trays of dainty food. "Soups and pastas are coming."

Josie looked at Sam, smiled, and picked up a fork. "I know this is going to be a lot easier—and more fun—than picking out a wedding dress."

Basil pulled a pen and notebook from his shirt pocket. "You two eat and enjoy. I'll keep track of what you do and don't want."

Josie and Sam managed to consume a huge meal during two hours of sipping and tasting Basil's best offerings. They left the restaurant and walked out into the moist night air, uncomfortably full and exhausted.

"Can you drive?" Josie asked, slipping into Sam's English leather seat and closing her eyes.

"I stopped drinking over an hour ago. What about you? I could drop you off at your apartment. Can you get a ride to work in the morning?"

"I think I'll be okay. After that first drink, I mostly just tasted the drinks. Really."

"If you're sure . . ."

It was only about twenty-five blocks, but Josie fell into a deep sleep, waking up with a start when Sam's wheel scraped against the curb in front of the Bride's Secret Bed and Breakfast. "Oh . . ."

"Are you sure you don't want a ride home?"

"I'm sure. I . . . what's the ringing?"

"My cell phone." Sam fumbled in his shirt pocket and answered. "It's my mother. She wants me to stop at the grocery store and pick up some butter—she's baking a cake."

"At this time of night? You don't think she's planning on baking our wedding cake, do you?"

"Anything is possible. I'd better get going. Summer hours are long, but I'm pretty sure the grocery closes at nine-thirty."

They kissed and Josie fumbled in her pockets for her truck keys as Sam roared off down the street. She was cursing her own inability to find a spot for her keys and stick to it when she appreciated her situation: if she hadn't spent those few minutes searching for the key, she might not have seen the flashlight beam as someone moved from room to room on the top floor of the Bride's Secret Bed and Breakfast.

TWENTY-SIX

A KEY TO the inn's front door was hanging on Josie's key ring, and she wasted no time getting into the house, taking care to leave the door open behind her. Leslie had switched off the circuit breakers on the first floor, but light from the street lamps streamed in through windows and the door, and she managed to reach the stairs without tripping over piled-up debris.

"Hello? Who's there?" she called out, beginning to mount the stairs. "This is a work site. It's dangerous to be here, and you're trespassing. Hello? Hello?"

Had she heard the click of a flashlight being turned off, or was her imagination working overtime? For the first time, Josie considered the possibility that she wasn't going to confront a teenager or two fooling around, possibly drinking or getting high, but someone whose intentions weren't so benign.

"Come on. It's time to get out. I won't call the police if you'll just leave so I can lock up, and we can all go home."

There was no answer, and Josie was wishing that she had thought to check the ground-floor doors and windows to figure out just how the intruder had gained entrance when she arrived on the second floor landing. She looked down the hallway to the right, and to the left, and was amazed to hear herself making a noise that belonged in a cheap horror movie.

The apparition at the end of the dark hall looked remarkably similar to photographs of the bride who had made the inn famous: dark blouse, flowing white skirt, long blond hair. But in a variation on the scary theme, the bride was carrying a gun pointed straight at Josie. She screamed again.

"For Pete's sake, shut up. Do you want the neighbors to call the station?"

It took a moment for Josie to recognize the voice and realize exactly whom she was seeing. "Officer Petric? Trish?"

"Who's there?"

"It's Josie. Josie Pigeon."

"Why did you scream?"

"I thought—I know this sounds stupid, but I thought you were the ghost—you know, the bride. The rumor on the island is that she walks the halls of this place at night," Josie explained, feeling like an idiot.

"Believe me, I'm no ghost. Why are you here?"

"I saw a light on the top floor and I was just checking it out. What about you?"

"I saw a light too—maybe the one you saw—but I've been through the entire building. If anyone was here, they're gone now." Trish was putting her gun back in her holster as she spoke. Josie's heart was still beating at double time, but she tried to sound in control.

"Yeah, maybe, but I suppose I'd better look around and see if the intruder took anything . . . Why are you carrying that dropcloth?" Trish, Josie realized, was wear-

ing her police uniform—that was the black shirt she had
seen—and carrying one of Island Contracting's heavy
cotton dropcloths, which Josie had seen as the floor-
length skirt the bride was supposed to have worn.

"I thought I heard something," Trish explained.

"Something hiding under the dropcloth?"

"It was draped over a sawhorse. I thought someone
might be hiding, crouched down behind it."

"Listen, my flashlight is out in my truck," Josie said,
not bothering to explain that its batteries were probably
dead. "Could you walk through the place with me while
I check everything out?" She didn't want to start messing
with circuit breakers—the last thing any of her workers
needed was an electrical surprise first thing tomorrow
morning.

"No problem. I wouldn't mind another look around
myself. We can start upstairs and work our way down."

"Great."

The women went through the house carefully, dis-
turbing some mice nibbling on old pizza crusts torn from
garbage bags on the top floor, closing a shutter that had
been blown open by the sea breezes, but discovering nothing out of order.

Josie was tired, and Trish didn't seem inclined to chat,
so they arrived back on the first floor having exchanged
few words. Josie was ready to lock up and go home when
the police woman spoke up.

"You grew up here, didn't you?"

"On the island? No. I moved here when I was in my
twenties, but I came here for family vacations when I
was a kid."

"Do you remember this place back then?"

"Not really. I think I heard the story of the bride's ghost, but I wasn't particularly interested. When I was young, all I cared about was swimming and crabbing. As a teenager, the romantic story might have appealed to me, but most of the time all I cared about was getting the perfect suntan—not easy for a redhead."

"I know what you mean. I burn easily, too."

Josie yawned. It seemed a bit late for small talk. "How do you think the intruder got in?"

"What intruder?"

"Whoever you saw," Josie explained. Apparently she wasn't the only exhausted person there. "In fact, how did you get in? I unlocked the front door."

"Through the back door—it was open."

"Really?"

"I should have said *unlocked*. I saw the light on the top floor, so I parked and checked all the doors. The door into the kitchen opened when I turned the knob, so I walked in to check things out . . . and probably scared away our intruder."

"Strange things seem to happen in this place," Josie commented, yawning again.

"You mean the murdered man."

"And those dummies that someone hid behind the walls—I've never seen anything like that. Although, of course, carpenters frequently find things people have stashed behind walls."

"Like what?"

"Notes, toys; I even found an old real estate sign behind the walls of a bathroom installed in the early fifties once. It's like signing wet cement—some people seem to feel the need to mark places where they have lived."

"Did you find anything like that here? Notes or anything?"

"Just the dummies—and they were enough."

"Yes, of course. I guess we'd better be going."

"Yeah, I need to go home and get some sleep. I guess you're still at work."

"Oh, yes. I'll circle the island a time or two and then head on back to the station."

"Great. I'll lock up the front if you'll make sure the back door is secure," Josie suggested.

"Great. See you."

"Yeah, see you." Josie left the Bride's Secret Bed and Breakfast, locking the front door behind her, and hurried back to her truck. She got in and drove off quickly, circling the block before parking and taking off on foot through the alley back to the Bride's Secret. She was in time to watch Officer Trish Petric check the latch on the back door, walk down the steps and stroll to her police car parked in the driveway of a nearby vacant home. The police officer looked around, got in her car and drove off—traveling, Josie noted, more than a few miles above the speed limit.

The evening had given Josie a lot to think about besides appetizers and alcoholic beverages. Trish Petric may have seen something suspicious in the Bride's Secret Bed and Breakfast, but her choice of parking place was equally suspect. Rental properties were frequently empty for weeks at a time; any police officer worth his or her salary would know which ones were unoccupied. By using the driveway of one of these homes, Trish had parked where no one would mind—and few would notice.

But why? The only reason Josie could come up with was that Trish had lied to her: her search of the Bride's Secret Bed and Breakfast had not been police business—at least not legitimate police business. Besides, if she had seen a light, why hadn't she called for backup instead of investigating on her own? Josie puzzled over this on the short drive to her apartment, but she arrived home with more questions than answers.

The sunroom where Risa spent much of the day smelled deliciously of an Italian feast as Josie passed through on her way to the stairs leading to her second-floor apartment. There was a note taped to her door, and she pulled it off to read in private. She headed straight for the small kitchen at one end of the large room where she and her son ate and lounged in front of the television. She realized she was actually hungry, and she unfolded the note as she opened her refrigerator door and peered inside. When she had left home that morning her refrigerator had contained a few out-of-date cartons of yogurt, an almost-empty quart of milk, some wilted carrots and squishy leaves of lettuce, and one very soft cantaloupe. It was now completely filled with Tupperware. Josie put down the sheet of paper unread and removed a few of the plastic rectangles. They were all labeled in Risa's flowery script: scungili in marinara sauce, homemade sausages with sweet peppers, sauces for pasta and polenta. Josie cracked open the lid of the squid, stuck in an exploratory finger, and tasted the contents. Delicious. Incredibly delicious. She pulled open a cupboard and located a plate, which she filled and placed in the microwave. As her snack heated, she cleared a spot on the counter so she could eat and read in comfort.

The note was from Risa and explained the stuffed refrigerator. Risa suggested Josie taste as many dishes as
she could and choose enough for a four-course traditional festive Italian meal. The squid, tender and delicious, satisfied Josie's stomach and her fatigue returned.
She placed the dirty dishes in the sink and headed for a
quick shower and bed.

"Mom? Do I smell food?"

Tyler wandered out of his room. He was wearing an
old pair of boxer shorts and a ragged Fish Wish Bait
Shop T-shirt. His red hair was tousled and he needed a
shave. His mother thought he looked adorable. "Are
you hungry?" she asked needlessly. Tyler was always
hungry.

"Starving."

Urchin jumped up on the counter and stretched a paw
toward the tomato-covered seafood.

"No, Urch." Tyler picked the cat up and dropped her
gently on the floor. "That's for us."

"Do you want the squid or something else? Risa has
left a ton of food here," Josie commented. Now that her
son was awake, she was discovering a second wind.

"Who do you think carried all this stuff up here?"
Tyler asked, opening the refrigerator door and peering
in. "I think veal meatballs and arugula sounds weird,
but it's really delish," he assured his mother. "I can heat
it myself," he added, popping the container in the microwave. "You and Sam were out late tonight," he commented sociably, opening the freezer and pulling out a
carton of ice cream to tide him over while his main
course heated.

"I stopped at the Bride's Secret on the way home,"
Josie explained.

"Any more dead bodies around?"

"No." Josie scratched Urchin's bony little head. "Tyler, what do you know about Officer Petric?"

"Why should I know anything about her?"

"I just thought you might. You always seem to hear things that I don't."

"We did talk once or twice," he admitted reluctantly. "I know that she summered on the island when she was a kid—like you did."

"Really? She's never mentioned that to me—not that we've had a lot of heart-to-heart conversations."

"Oh? Well, she had relatives here, and she stayed with them. But I don't know much more than that. She did say that there was only one pizza place here back then."

Josie smiled. "Guess those weren't the good old days."

"Yeah, can you imagine the long line of people waiting for pies on weekends?"

"I wonder if Chief Rodney worked here then."

"Yeah, maybe he gave her tickets and now she gives other people tickets . . . that would be weird."

"I suppose."

Tyler pulled a hot dish from the microwave with his fingertips and slid it down on the table. "There is one thing I don't get about her."

"What's that?"

"She just happened to mention to me once that she was first in her graduating class at the police academy."

"Good for her. What don't you get?"

"I don't get why she's working here when she could have gone anywhere."

Half an hour later Tyler's question was one of the three keeping Josie awake. The other two were why

Trish hadn't mentioned summering on the island as a child when she and Josie were talking about their childhoods, and how could Josie possibly explain to Risa or Basil that she had chosen one and not the other to cater her wedding reception?

TWENTY-SEVEN

THE PRESENCE OF home owners rarely improves a work site—at least in the opinion of contractors and their crews. An architect's appearance can bring with it problems or solutions. Unfortunately, Christopher and his grandmother walked into the Bride's Secret Bed and Breakfast a second or two after the elegant mahogany wainscoting in the living room had separated from the cracking plaster and smashed onto the floor.

"I thought your plans called for that lovely old wood remaining in place, dear," Tilly Higgins said, looking at Christopher through the plaster dust.

"They do, Grandmother."

"The plaster was separating from the old lathes. This way we can replaster the walls and refinish that old mahogany before reinstalling it," Josie spoke up, hoping the old mahogany hadn't been damaged beyond repair in its sudden contact with the floor.

"Do you think perhaps you should move it?" Tilly asked, waving her hand before her face.

"Moving it will stir up more dust—maybe you would prefer my crew to wait until you've left the building?" Josie asked.

"I think that's an excellent idea," Christopher said,

taking his grandmother's arm and leading her toward the stairway. "We're here to walk through the bedrooms and bathrooms on the second and third floors."

"And closets. I don't think your grandfather has any idea about closets," Tilly added. "Every time I mention adding storage, he just says it's under control, don't worry, there will be plenty of space for everything. I'd like to see for myself while I'm here."

"Actually, he was here checking storage in the bedrooms a few days ago," Josie pointed out, relieved that the subject had been changed. She would wait until they were alone to examine the woodwork more closely. "Did your grandfather talk to you about the possibility of adding to the master bedroom suite and decreasing the size of the room next door?" she asked Christopher.

"He said something about it on the phone, I think. I've been away visiting my old roommate's family cottage up in Maine for a bit of sailing and clam digging."

"Poor Christopher works so hard during the school year; he certainly deserves a break this summer. I always say summer isn't summer unless there's an opportunity to take a nice vacation, don't you?"

Josie didn't answer. She didn't want Christopher hanging around and looking over her shoulder constantly, but she worked hard—harder than most students, she suspected—and she hadn't had a summer vacation in decades. "Well, your husband thinks that adding storage to the master bedroom suite is worth giving up some space in the smaller suite next door."

"Seymour is always complaining about my clothing. He thinks a woman can own a half dozen or so outfits and then somehow manage to appear perfectly dressed on all occasions. He's always telling me how his mother owned one little black dress that she dressed up or dressed down with a few accessories. Completely absurd. The woman's jewels and furs were famous from Manhattan to Paris. No one even noticed what she was wearing underneath all that glitter and hair most of the time."

"Did she vacation here?" Josie asked.

"Lord, no. She hated the beach—so much sand and surf—unless it was in Nassau or Bermuda or possibly the South of France, and she was looking at it out the window of a deluxe hotel suite. But she believed in work—for everyone other than herself—and insisted on Seymour having summer jobs, which is how he ended up here."

"Grandfather is always saying that he inherited a fortune and was taught a work ethic," Christopher commented.

Josie had a work ethic, but she wasn't sure whether or not it would have been quite so strong if she had been lucky enough to inherit a fortune. "What sort of fortune? I mean, where did the money come from?" she asked.

"Seymour's family was in banking and securities, but Seymour has been diversifying since he took over running the firm. Seymour has a talent for putting together many different pieces and turning them into a successful whole. Higgins International has a finger in many pies," Tilly explained.

"Oh."

"Just what is that thing doing there?" Tilly asked, frowning. She was pointing to the dropcloth Trish had left on the floor the night before. Josie looked down at it. Had someone moved the dropcloth since then? She was about to wonder what that might mean, when the door at the end of the hall leading to the attic opened and Leslie appeared, a dozen bulging plastic bags cradled in his arms.

"Hi, boss!" He spoke to Josie, but directed his charm at Tilly Higgins.

Mrs. Higgins, a woman who, Josie suspected, got through much of her life by displaying her own considerable supply of charm, didn't bother to respond in kind. "What do you have there?" she asked abruptly.

Leslie glanced down at his laden arms before answering. "Garbage. Mostly old knob-and-tube wiring that should have been removed up there long ago."

Josie opened her mouth to make a comment and then shut it without speaking. Leslie was lying. This place had been rewired decades before. Knob-and-tube wiring was something no insurance company would ignore. Josie didn't know what was going on, and she was determined to find out. But she didn't feel the need to share her problem with her employer. "Leslie, when you get back from the Dumpster, give Mary Ann a hand with the last window at the end of the second floor corridor, will you? Nic and Vicki have almost finished ripping the tiles out of the bathrooms on that floor."

"No problem."

Josie's cell phone rang as Leslie galloped down the stairs. "Excuse me, but this might be about your tile order," she said, pulling the phone from her pocket.

"I was thinking about those tiles, Christopher," Tilly said as they walked off down the hallway. "Perhaps those glass ones are not the look we want. One of my friends has some wonderful hand-painted Italian tiles on the walls of her guest bath . . ."

Josie answered her phone, hoping Christopher was explaining to his grandmother that changing her tile order would cost extra money—and might delay the whole project. "Hi. Josie Pigeon here."

Betty was on the other end of the line, but Josie's smile faded as she heard the reason for her friend's call. "Son of a gun. Are you sure?" Josie listened to her friend's answer and a few new examples of JJ's brilliance before hanging up, tucking the phone back in her pocket, and heading off to see what Christopher and his grandmother were doing. Betty had given her something new to think about: according to Seymour Higgins's granddaughter, one of the "pies" in which her grandfather had a finger was the insurance company that had just raised Island Contracting's premiums.

Josie went to join Christopher and his grandmother with a few questions of her own. But their questions had priority and Josie had to explain over and over that while the changes that Christopher wanted might, yes, improve the final result, they would cost more—much more—than the budget they had agreed on. Under normal circumstances, Josie felt uncomfortable asking for more money, but now, considering her insurance company's lack of hesitation on that score—and its relationship to the Higgins family fortune—she casually mentioned a few tens of thousands of dollars.

Tilly Higgins blew up. "I don't understand you tradespeople!" she said in response to Josie's explanation of the difference in cost between a new wood floor and custom-cut tilework. "You lay out the price of a job, and once it has begun and everything is demolished, you begin adding to the cost of the job. It's unconscionable. When I go to Barney's for a sweater, I pay the price on the tag. If you were running the store, I would end up paying ten . . . fifteen . . . even twenty percent more! I don't understand how you think you can get away with these casual markups."

"If you went to Barney's and instead of buying a plain sweater, you bought one with a mink collar, you would expect to pay more, right?" Josie asked, working to keep her voice level.

"I would never buy a sweater with a mink collar—too tacky—and besides, I already own three mink coats. Why would I want a sweater with a fur collar?"

"That might not be the best example," Josie began again. "But the point I'm making is that you changed the plans, so of course you would expect to pay more when you are asking for more."

"My husband is not going to understand this sort of thing. I had to talk him into buying this place. It's important that the remodeling goes smoothly and doesn't end up costing more than the price we have agreed on. Dear Seymour is so worried about money these days."

"Are you saying that your husband doesn't change the prices of things himself? I think I can tell you that, in fact . . ."

"I am not going to stand here and argue with you over these things. I told Seymour that we should hire a bigger contracting company, but he insisted on your little business doing the job. And now, of course, with that body turning up . . . well, you should be glad that the island police have allowed you to continue working here. If Seymour hadn't intervened, you might be standing in line for unemployment benefits right this minute!"

"I . . . I might what?" But Josie's words were spoken to Tilly's back as she stalked down the hall.

"Christopher, you deal with this. I'm late for tennis,"

she called over her shoulder as she started down the stairs.

"My grandmother is a bit sensitive about money these days," Christopher explained quietly. "Grandfather was more than a little upset when she bought herself that new BMW convertible without talking it over with him. And she had the kitchen in their townhouse remodeled only a few months ago."

"But I'm only trying to charge for changes she has made."

"That's the problem, you see. If he had wanted the changes made, he'd be happy to pay for them."

"And what did she mean about your grandfather intervening in the police investigation of the murder?" Josie asked.

"Grandfather put pressure on the local police force to . . . to keep their investigation away from this building, I guess is how he explained it."

"I don't get it. What are you saying?"

"Just that Grandfather is anxious to be in this house by the end of the summer."

"He's made that plain more than once," Josie said.

"And he was worried that a full-scale investigation into the murder might cause delays in our schedule."

"Not nearly as much as all the changes your grandmother wants to make," Josie pointed out.

"But he doesn't know about them yet, does he? Anyway, I don't really know what happened—or if anything happened, I guess. But Grandmother said that he had made sure the island police stayed away from the Bride's Secret Bed and Breakfast after the body was found here."

"Really? And your grandmother told you that?"

"Yes, at breakfast this morning. She's just as anxious

as he is to have this project completed on time. She's already busy picking out furniture and curtains and stuff. She's even spoken with a friend who has a niece who is an editor at *Elle Décor,* and has convinced her that this place might be worth a story in their magazine next spring."

"But the island police . . ."

"Apparently Grandfather spoke with your local police chief and the man was willing to make sure his investigation didn't interfere with our work. He probably made a sizable contribution to the island police benevolent society—or whatever you have here. That's the way Grandfather usually works."

"And why shouldn't he, when he can get that money by simply charging someone else an exorbitant premium for services?"

"Excuse me? I don't follow that."

"It doesn't matter right now," she answered, furious. "Look, I have things to do. Could you make a list of all your grandmother's changes and whether you think we can talk her out of them? I'll take a look later this afternoon and we can discuss it—as well as a few problems that we're having . . ."

"What?"

"Nothing serious. Some of the lights could be installed more cheaply if we didn't have to cross beams, and what do you want to do about access to the plumbing once we close up the walls? Little stuff like that. Are you going to be around later?"

"Sure. Let me give you my cell phone number and you can give me a call."

"Great."

Josie was in her truck on the way to the police station

before it occurred to her that what she had just learned might explain Trish Petric's presence at the Bride's Secret the night before. Perhaps that young officer had been investigating the murder on her own, since the Rodneys apparently had been bribed to leave the murder unsolved.

TWENTY-EIGHT

T HE LOCAL POLICE department had offices in the large brick municipal building located near the center of the island. Josie parked in the macadam parking lot, skirted the long line of tourists waiting to buy beach passes in the booth provided, and entered the lobby where Officer Petric sat, perched on the edge of the dispatcher's desk.

Mrs. Tracy Pepper, who worked as the weekday dispatcher in the summer and returned to her job as an elementary school secretary the rest of the year, looked up and smiled. "Josie Pigeon. I was just talking about you over the weekend. Word on the island is that you and Sam are going to have the wedding to end all weddings. Did I hear a rumor about twelve bridesmaids?"

"You may have heard that, but all I can say is you can't believe everything you hear," Josie answered.

"Well, I sure hope you don't forget my husband and me—we wouldn't want to miss the sight of Tyler in a tuxedo escorting you down the aisle. Which church have you reserved, by the way? The Catholic church is the biggest, of course, but I think the Episcopal has the most charm. On the other hand, the Methodist church has that large hall for the reception. You know all your guests will hang around for that if Risa is going to be catering. What do you think?"

"I'm letting Sam decide on the church," Josie said, dropping that problem right in her fiancé's lap. She realized Trish Petric was staring at her. "Good to see you again," Josie said.

Trish just nodded, not bothering to put a smile on her face.

"Officer Petric and I ran into each other in the middle of the night at the Bride's Secret Bed and Breakfast," Josie said to Mrs. Pepper.

"I will be filing a report, if you're interested in all the details," Trish explained, sliding off the desk. "I'm going to hit the road. Good to see you again," she said over her shoulder as she marched to the door.

"She's not very friendly, is she?" Josie asked when she and the dispatcher were alone together in the lobby.

"Well, not to you, that's for sure. I haven't had any complaints. She's certainly quite competent. Does her work well, fills out reports on time—which is more than I can say for the Rodneys," she added, lowering her voice to a whisper. "Sometimes this office runs weeks behind when it comes to paperwork. You would be amazed."

"Not really," Josie admitted. "Remember, I was once young and foolish enough to date Mike, and he used to brag about taking the long view and not getting bogged down in petty details. I sort of guessed that meant he didn't fill out a lot of forms in a timely fashion." Josie didn't mention that she hated paperwork as well.

"Well, Officer Petric is a real addition to the department." Mrs. Pepper looked at the closed door that led to the police department offices. "Are you here about the construction job?"

"You mean the murdered man at the Bride's Secret?"

"No." She turned her back and began to go through files in the bottom drawer of her desk. "I mean the new forensic center."

"The what?"

"The new forensic center." The dispatcher didn't raise her voice, but she enunciated as clearly as possible.

"What new forensic center?"

"The one that's going to be built over the winter—don't tell me you haven't heard about it yet!"

"No. Is the state going to locate a new laboratory in the area?"

"It has nothing to do with the state. The island police department is going to have its very own forensic laboratory—I should say laboratories. But I probably shouldn't have mentioned them to you. The public announcement hasn't been made."

"I certainly haven't heard anything about it," Josie said. "Do you have any idea where the money is coming from?"

"The rumor is a private donor, but that doesn't mean anything, does it?" She looked up, an indignant expression on her face. "And when I consider how much is really needed here on the island—wouldn't you think that anyone wanting to contribute to the community would realize we need a new playground at the elementary school more than a forensic lab? I mean, the only real crimes we have here are the bodies that keep turning up on Island Contracting's work sites . . . not that anyone blames you, of course."

Josie had been ready to confront the Rodneys about this new rumor, but she decided there was more to learn here first. Mrs. Pepper not only kept her ear to the ground, but she answered the phone: she was in a unique position to know more about what was going on than most. And she might be convinced to share her information with the mother of one of her all-time favorite students. "There's no evidence connecting anyone working for Island Contracting with the dead man," Josie pointed out.

"Except that good-looking electrician—wasn't his driver's license found on the corpse?"

"Yes. But he didn't know the man."

"Of course that's what he would say."

"Do you know something I don't know?" Josie asked.

"He had all those speeding tickets, and he didn't pay some of the fines—that's illegal—and it's not at all honest. I don't know about you, but I would have a hard time trusting someone like that."

Josie remembered the bags Leslie had been hauling from the attic. By coming down here she may have missed the opportunity to identify their contents. Contents about which Leslie certainly had lied. "Yes. You're right there," she said. "But I thought it was odd that Leslie was brought down here yesterday just to be asked about the tickets. I mean, he said that no one asked him about the murdered man. Of course, he could have lied," she added.

"Nope. He was almost arrested over those tickets." Again Tracy lowered her voice and leaned closer to Josie. "If you ask me there was something odd about that—it didn't make any sense. And I'm not the only person who thinks so."

"Who else?"

"Officer Petric was outraged—literally outraged—by the whole thing."

"Really?'

"Yup. She could hardly talk, she was so angry. She stood right where you're standing right now and told me that she was thinking of quitting the force over it all."

"Really?"

"Yes. But she's young and idealistic. I pointed out that leaving her first job without a good recommendation might affect her entire career, and that she would do more good by working hard this summer and learning from the experience."

"And she agreed with you?"

"Well, she's still here, isn't she?"

"Yeah. Did you know that Officer Petric used to spend summers here when she was young?"

"Of course I did. I didn't understand why she would take this job, to tell the truth, but she explained that she had ties to the island that went way back. Her being here made more sense after I understood that. She's so smart—first in her class at the police academy and in college, I understand—there had to be a reason why she would turn up on the island working for our police department." Mrs. Pepper looked over Josie's shoulder and smiled. "Chief Rodney . . . I was just about to make some coffee. Perhaps you would like a cup?"

"Is that why you're here, Miss Pigeon? Looking for a free cup of coffee?"

"No, Chief Rodney, but I do want to talk to you."

"Then step into my office. We can have some privacy. No point in the entire island knowing our business, is there, Mrs. Pepper?"

"Definitely not, Chief Rodney." The dispatcher waited until the police chief's back was turned to wink at Josie, who smiled back and then followed the man through the doorway to his office.

"So, what can I do for you, Miss Pigeon?"

"I . . ."

"Other than offer Island Contracting the job of a lifetime, that is."

"What are you talking about?"

"Come now, Josie, I know you and Mrs. Pepper are thick as thieves. I can't imagine that you and she have been talking out there for . . ." He glanced down at his watch. "For almost five minutes without her spilling the beans about the new forensic laboratory that is going to be built right here on the island."

"How did you know I'd been here for five minutes?"

Chief Rodney pointed to the television monitor Josie had noticed the last time she was here. This time it was on and broadcasting a clear view of the dispatcher's desk as well as the front door. "New security cameras. Our little island got its share of funds from the Department of Homeland Security, same as the big cities."

Josie turned, looked up, and together they watched a young woman and a small child walk through the police station doors, cross the lobby, and speak to Mrs. Pepper. The dispatcher waved in the direction of the rest rooms and the visitors took off.

"Gotta remember to remind that Pepper woman that these rest rooms are not for the general public—only people here on official police business," Chief Rodney growled.

"No audio?" Josie asked.

"No, we were gonna get it, but it turned out to be too expensive."

"Sound was too expensive but you're talking about

funding a new forensics laboratory?" Josie asked, relieved that her conversation with the dispatcher hadn't been overheard.

"Different funds. Wait until the island sees what's going to be built in that empty lot behind the old water tower." He pulled rolled blueprints from beneath his desk and began to spread them out. "Look at this."

She looked—and marveled. "This is incredible. Do I count six laboratories?"

"Seven. And nine offices, and three men's rooms and one ladies' room. Not bad, right?"

"Incredible," she repeated. "Where did the money come from?"

"Private donor. Wants to remain anonymous. You know how it is."

"Not really, but I'd sure like to find out." Josie leaned closer, examining the handwritten instructions concerning under-floor plumbing requirements. "So when is this project going to be up for bids?"

"What bids? I'm not following you, Miss Pigeon."

"I assume bidding for this project will be open to all the contractors on the island."

"No . . ."

"And off-island, I suppose," she added, thinking she had made a mistake.

"You're missing the point, Miss Pigeon. The anonymous donor has already picked a contractor—and you're it."

"Island Contracting's going to build this?"

"You got it."

"It doesn't have to be bidded out?"

"Nope. And there's a contract ready to be signed just

as soon as you're finished with your summer project. All nice and legal. Congratulations."

"I . . . I don't know what to say," she started before another thought struck. "This is being done on the cheap, right? I can't afford to take on a job that might end up costing me money."

"Nope. The anonymous donor has been real generous. What do you think about . . . for the job," he added, naming a figure.

"I think it's fantastic. Maybe too fantastic to be believed," she added.

"You believe it, Josie Pigeon. Sounds to me like this may be your lucky year."

"Yeah, courtesy of your anonymous donor," Josie said, turning and looking back up at the security monitor. Christopher Higgins had just walked in the front door of the station house with his grandfather—better known in this room, at least, as the anonymous donor.

TWENTY-NINE

"**L**OOKS LIKE YOU have company—the architect of your new forensic laboratory and his grandfather, who I assume donated the money for your building," Josie pointed out.

"Damn it, Josie, why do you think you know who donated the money for this project?"

"I recognized the handwriting on the blues you just showed me. I should—Christopher keeps changing the ones I'm using to remodel his grandfather's house."

"And Seymour Higgins must be happy with your work since, as you have guessed, he insisted on hiring Island Contracting for this project."

"We do excellent work for a reasonable price."

"Yeah, but you're a real pain in the butt, Josie. I told him that there were other companies, but he insisted on you." Chief Rodney shrugged. "You know what they say: never look a gift horse in the mouth."

"So I've heard. . . . They're leaving," Josie said, surprised.

"Probably here to drop off some papers—that Seymour Higgins must spend a fortune on lawyers. There are always more papers to sign. I've wasted many precious hours on that man."

"But anything for a forensic laboratory, right?" Josie knew she sounded sarcastic, and apparently Chief Rodney heard it too.

"This is a big deal, Josie. And it's important to me for reasons other than the fact that it will be a tribute to my years—my decades—running this police department."

"Don't tell me your name is going to be on the building. I don't believe it!"

"I suggested the Rodney and Higgins Forensic Center, or even the Higgins and Rodney Forensic Center, but Mr. Higgins . . . Seymour . . . insisted on the Rodney Island Forensic Center."

"So you expect the island to be named after you as well?" Josie asked. "And who the hell thinks we need a forensic center—or even a single laboratory—here anyway?"

"If we had a forensic laboratory here we might know who the dead man is," Chief Rodney replied. "And how the hell can anyone figure out who killed the man unless we can identify him, I'd like to know."

"Still no identification? Really?"

"Nope. No one matching his description has disappeared in the last month or so. A photograph was distributed nationally, but not a word. We could have a dangerous serial killer loose on the island and without that laboratory, there's no goddamn way we're gonna know it."

"A serial killer who dresses up his victims as brides? Doesn't that sound just a bit unlikely to you?"

"You think serial killers are sane? Do you have any idea of the strange ritual tortures some of them inflict on their victims? Why just last night on television there was a show about sexual deviancy, and . . ."

"I don't want to hear about it, Chief. Really I don't."

"Well if you watched shows like that you might understand why we need a forensic laboratory here."

"Look, I'm not gonna argue with you. All of this comes as a complete surprise to me. And as for building a forensic laboratory—well, I don't even know if I want to be working for Seymour Higgins again. And I won't know until I've finished up this project."

Chief Rodney frowned. "It would be very, very foolish of you to turn down his generous offer, and it might screw up the entire goddamn project. You wouldn't want to do that, would you?"

Josie recognized the worried expression on his face and worked to keep from smiling. She could screw this up if she turned down the contract! The smile escaped and she beamed. For the first time in the years since she had been living on the island, Josie Pigeon had the upper hand when it came to dealing with the Rodneys. "I'll have to examine the contract very carefully," she explained and turned to leave the room. "And we'll have to agree—in writing—to a minimum of interference from . . . your office," she added as she made her exit.

The door slammed behind her and Tracy Pepper looked up. "Josie, you make that man angrier than anyone on the island."

"Yeah, well, his son hates me even more," Josie pointed out.

"True."

"I suppose I'd better be getting back to work. Now that I know Chief Rodney can see everything that goes on out here, I feel sort of self-conscious."

"That damn camera bugged the hell out of me until I

realized he couldn't see anything I didn't want him to see."

"What do you mean?"

"Notice where the file cabinets are?"

Josie looked over in the corner and smiled. "So when you're going through the files . . ."

"I can't be seen on camera, and no one else can either."

"But . . ."

"And some residents have begun using the back door to come and go as well. It's more convenient if you park in the back lot," the dispatcher pointed out.

"And can't be seen on camera, either."

"Got it in one. In fact, I've recently noticed that Trish Petric prefers that particular entrance."

"Really?"

"And someone else uses it, although he doesn't come down the station all that frequently."

"Who?"

"Sam Richardson. In fact, he stopped in and asked me to tell you that he's waiting in the parking lot for you."

"How did he know I was here?"

"Could be that red Island Contracting truck parked out front."

Josie grinned. "Yeah, I suppose that could be it. While I was talking with Chief Rodney, Seymour Higgins and his grandson were here, right?"

"Sure were. They dropped a bunch of papers off for the chief to sign."

"That's what Chief Rodney said."

"Damn that man and his camera. It's fine if he wants to see who is coming and going, but why does he think he has a right to spy on me? I'm thinking of having a torrid affair right in the middle of my desk—give him something interesting to watch."

"That might take his mind off last night's television, for sure," Josie said. She added a good-bye, agreed to tell Tyler that his old school secretary was asking after him, and waving to Chief Rodney, left the building by the front door.

She hurried around to the back, where Sam Richardson was sitting in his MGB, top down, face up to the sun.

"Sam, I'm so glad you're here. You won't believe what has happened!"

"Something good, I hope!"

"Something amazing, but I have to get back to work."

"Josie . . ."

"The truck is out front."

"I know. That's how I found you. I was over at the Bride's Secret and everything was going just fine," Sam paused and fingered a lock of her hair, "but I have something to show you. And if I'm right, things may not be quite so fine after I do."

Sam had her complete attention. "What do you mean? What's wrong?"

"I think I should show you rather than tell you. Let's go to my house."

"Sam, I have to work."

"I know. But this will be time well spent, unless I'm wrong—and I really don't think I am."

"Okay. But I'll drive my truck. That way I can leave from there and not waste any more time."

"You got it." He started his engine. "Meet you there in ten minutes."

Josie nodded and hurried back to her truck. She drove to Sam's place, her worry about what he was going to show her replacing the joy at having a large winter building project fall into her company's lap.

Sam had bought one of the few ranch houses built in the dunes in the 1950s. Except for the addition of a deck across the front of the home, which Josie had hated until Hurricane Agatha tore it off, he had done nothing to modernize the place. And he wouldn't. Sam loved the 1950s and 1960s, and the entire postwar look, as much as Josie hated it. But she didn't have time to think about their divergent tastes. Sam had left his front door open, and Josie entered and found him hunched over his computer. She walked across the room and looked over his shoulder.

"You're shopping on eBay? I got the impression that you wanted to show me something important."

"I did and I do. Look at this."

"An incredibly ugly chair."

"Vintage California design," he said. "And look at this one."

"I don't . . ."

"Keep looking," he ordered and scrolled down the screen. "Think, Josie, haven't you seen these things before?"

"Not those exactly, but I've seen chairs like them here in your house. And those white Plexiglas chairs look like the ones that were in the dining room at the Bride's Secret."

"How many were there?"

"Twelve."

"There are twelve for sale here . . ."

But Josie was still browsing. "Look at that hideous

buffet—it looks like one that was in the living room at the Bride's Secret. And those white lamps, they're like the ones that were in the foyer." She stopped speaking as Sam pointed to the next item for sale. "That looks just like the dresser that those lamps were sitting on. Sam, this is the furniture from the Bride's Secret Bed and Breakfast."

"Is that what it looks like to you?"

She looked again. "Yes. Is that what it looks like to you?"

Sam smiled grimly. "Yes. That's exactly what it looks like to me."

"But how did you find it?"

"I was just killing time this morning, looking for some mid-century antiques."

"Where are you going to put any more furniture? Your place is jammed."

"That's not important now. What I'm trying to tell you is that I came upon a Holmegaard lamp that looked like one you moved just a few weeks ago. And then there was this chair . . . and this vinyl couch . . . and this . . . and this . . . ."

"All from the Bride's Secret?"

"Well, I wasn't sure about that immediately, but then I looked more closely and discovered something very interesting."

"What?"

"The pieces I thought I recognized—the ones you just recognized—are all being sold by the same person."

"Not one of the Higgins family, I gather."

"No, the person selling these things is using ZapU as his or her screen name."

"Who?"

"ZapU." Sam spelled it out. "I didn't get it for a minute and then I realized it could be . . ."

"An electrician! It's Leslie! That's what he was doing this morning—carrying more things out of the house to sell!"

"What things?"

"I don't know what it was—everything was stuffed into black plastic garbage bags. He said it was old knob-and-tube wiring, but all that crap was removed years and years ago. I'm sure about that."

"So you knew he was lying."

"Yes."

"What did you say to him?"

"Nothing. Tilly Higgins and Christopher were with me. I have a policy of keeping problems with employees within the company and away from our employers."

"Good policy, but you know you can't ignore this now."

"No, of course not. But how can I prove that this ZapU is really Leslie?"

Sam was scrolling through his screen. "No problem. Let's see, there's a seller's profile here somewhere—here. Look. New seller. Unrated. Lives less than twenty miles from here as well."

"Unrated? You're saying he hasn't done this before."

"Not using this name, but you know how it is with computers—you can drop or pick up a new screen name almost any time you wish just by signing up for a new service."

"Yeah, I guess."

"Yeah definitely. Leslie could do this every time he

works on a new job. Josie, speeding might not be the only illegal habit Leslie Coyne has."

She stared at the screen and tried to absorb what Sam was saying. "I need an electrician on this job—I costed it out with a minimum of subcontractors—and he's an excellent worker and a more-than-competent carpenter."

"As well as a hard worker if he heads home at night and sells things on eBay. It's not just taking photos, writing up descriptions, and setting up an account before you list items that takes work. It's also packing up the goods and mailing them out once they're sold. There are entire companies set up so that people can sell things without all the work that goes along with it. Leslie has been one busy young man."

"If this is Leslie. You're basing all this on circumstantial evidence—the name, the location, the fact that this seller has no history. We haven't proved anything yet."

"Well, then let's prove it." Sam scrolled through the items for sale. "Like this lamp?"

"It's certainly bright," Josie said, staring at the brilliant indigo glass base shaped like a teardrop and topped with a torn ivory linen shade.

"It will look better with a new shade. In fact, it will look perfect next to the bed in the guest room. I'll offer to pay more than it's worth and see if the seller is willing to end the auction and sell to me."

"And then?"

"And then I'll explain that I'm from the city and at the shore—not on this island—for a few weeks and offer to meet and pick it up. Between the high price and the fact that Leslie—or whoever—won't have to bother packing and shipping, I think we may flush out our seller."

"I suppose it's worth a try," Josie said. She wondered if they actually had to use the lamp once they bought it, but decided this wasn't the time to have an argument over a difference in taste.

"Okay. I'll make a very generous offer," Sam said as his mother joined them.

"Sammy, I saw Josie's truck out front—is she here?"

"I am, Carol, but not for long. What's wrong?"

Sam's mother was flushed and obviously very upset. "I've just had terrible news!" she explained, running her hands through her well-lacquered hair.

Sam jumped up. "Are you okay? Has someone died?"

"No, but . . . it's Josie. My dear, my friend Gert just called with the total bill for your wedding gown." Carol held a slip of paper in her hand and Josie reached for it. "Before you look, I want you to promise me that you will allow this dress to be my gift to you."

"I don't think . . ." Josie looked at the number and gasped. "I know I can't spend this amount on a dress, and I won't let you, either."

"But . . ."

"Carol. I'm sure about this. I just wrote a check for that amount recently—it paid my increased insurance premium for Island Contracting—and I had to struggle to pay that. I can't spend that type of money on a dress that I will only wear for one day. Period."

Sam looked at his mother. "Perhaps you might switch to plan two," he suggested gently.

THIRTY

SAM HAD WORKED late into the night to discover the identity of ZapU. His last phone call to Josie had awakened her around three A.M. Sam explained that he had left messages for ZapU all over the Internet and he would call Josie just as soon as he received a reply. Josie drove to work in a fog. She needed to know if Leslie was selling property he had stolen from the Bride's Secret Bed and Breakfast on eBay, but she also wondered if she could get him to set the caps for lights on the first floor before she was forced to fire him. Hurrying up the front steps to the work site, she was so busy thinking about this situation that it took her a few minutes to realize that her crew was busy too—discussing her son.

"Tyler couldn't have been sweeter, but I certainly don't understand what his teachers are thinking of," Nic was saying.

"I know what you mean, I thought anthropologists studied primitive tribes in places like Africa," Vicki interrupted.

"Maybe you ladies are closer to those tribes than you realize," Leslie suggested.

"That may be, but I finally had to tell him that the only way I could make sure I had all the places and dates absolutely correct was to check my resumé—and then he asked for a copy of it. He said it would make a great footnote. I sure never expected to be in a footnote!" Mary Ann said.

Both Vicki and Nic were laughing at Mary Ann's tale, and even Leslie was leaning against the wall with a broad grin on his face when Josie entered the room.

"When did you all talk to Tyler?" she asked abruptly. "And why?"

Complete silence greeted her appearance, and no one seemed anxious to answer her questions. Nic and Mary Ann found something to stare at on the floor while Vicki and Leslie focused on each other.

"We're not supposed to tell you," Mary Ann finally said, looking up.

"He wanted it to be a surprise," Vicki added.

"Wanted what to be a surprise?" Josie asked.

"It's his senior project," Nic answered after another long lull. "He's studying us."

"Not just us, there are other women too," Vicki said.

"Women who work on the island," Mary Ann continued. "He's thinking of studying anthropology in college and his adviser at school suggested that he might want to fashion a senior project around a small society. At least I think that's what he said . . ."

"Anyway, what we're trying to say is that your son is spending his summer studying the working women on this island," Nic said.

"And that includes us," Vicki said.

"And that includes Officer Trish Petric, doesn't it?" Josie asked slowly.

"Probably does," Nic answered.

"But you're not going to ask him a lot of questions about it, are you?" Vicki asked.

"The kid really wants to keep it a secret from you," Leslie pointed out.

"But why?" Josie asked.

"He wants to surprise you with the finished project. He explained that it's sort of a tribute to you—to all the years you've worked without recognition," Mary Ann said. She smiled. "You must know how proud he is of the way you've created a life for yourself and for him."

"I . . . I suppose." Josie felt herself tearing up. "So how did he manage to talk to you all without me knowing about it?" she asked a bit gruffly.

"He arranged for you to be out of town, in New York City buying your wedding dress," Vicki answered.

"I'm not going to buy that dress," Josie began. "Wait a second, are you telling me that Tyler orchestrated my shopping trip to New York?"

"Apparently he's friends with the waitress who works the breakfast shift at Sullivan's," Mary Ann explained.

"Tyler asked that young woman to talk about going to New York and buying a wedding gown while I was eating breakfast there?"

Her crew was grinning as Nic answered. "Yeah, that's exactly what he did. He wanted to talk to us all without you around, so he arranged for you to be someplace else. He even said he had a backup plan if that one didn't work. Pretty smart, huh?"

Josie frowned. "Yeah, I guess."

"So you've got a smart son who appreciates all you've given him. Why do you look so unhappy?" Nic asked.

"Because Tyler's not the only person who has been

manipulating me." Josie thought about this for a moment while her crew waited for her continue.

"From the beginning of this job things have been happening that I can't explain . . . not just the dummies appearing and the murder, but other things like our insurance situation. I hire new crews all the time and this isn't the first time my insurance company has questioned me about workers, but this is the first time that the problems appeared so quickly or were so impossible to resolve. And then there have been so many problems with the police . . ." She looked at her crew. "What Tyler's been doing may have been manipulative, but it was for a good cause—he was working on his project and trying to be nice to me. But I think the killer has been manipulating me—and you all—and the police—for a different reason. He's been trying to protect himself."

Vicki gasped and Leslie put his arms around her.

"You know who the killer is?" Nic asked.

"Yes. I do." Josie reached up and pushed her hair off her forehead. "I don't know why the man was killed. I don't even know who the dead man is. But I do know who killed him." Josie looked around the Bride's Secret Bed and Breakfast, a sad expression on her face. "I don't like it though. Not one bit."

Before anyone could ask anything else, Josie's cell phone rang. Sam was calling with the news that Leslie was, in fact, selling the contents of the Bride's Secret Bed and Breakfast on eBay, using ZapU as his screen name. Sometime in the early morning, Leslie had answered a couple of the messages Sam had left for him, and he had identified himself. Josie thanked Sam for getting to the bottom of that problem, said she was busy and would call him later, and flipped her phone shut without mentioning her new suspicions.

Then she took a deep breath and straightened out her shoulders. She was going to do something she hated to do, something she usually worked hard to avoid doing: she was going to go talk with the island police. She had spent way too much time with them in the past few weeks, but she didn't see that she had any other option.

Josie drove to the police station, reviewing what she believed to be facts. By the time she was parking in the lot by the municipal building, she knew what she had to say and she knew how to say it. She walked into the police station through the front door, resisting an urge to wave at the surveillance camera pointed in her direction. Trish Petric was sitting in the chair behind the dispatcher's desk; she looked up and smiled as the door swung closed behind Josie.

"Is Chief Rodney in?" Josie asked.

"Yes." Trish pointed at the monitor. "And he probably knows you're here now, too. If you're trying to avoid him, you should have used the back door," the officer added.

Josie half-smiled. Now that she knew why Tyler had been talking with Trish Petric in her patrol car, her antagonism had disappeared. "Actually, I want to talk to him . . . and you too, if it's possible."

"I'm stuck here while the regular dispatcher is at the dentist, but she's due back any time now. Do you think your business with the chief will take more than a few minutes?"

"That depends on whether or not he believes me," Josie answered. "If you'll just come back when you're free?" She opened the door to the offices at the rear of the building, then stopped and asked a question.

"Officer Petric, do you know if Seymour Higgins has ever been stopped for speeding on the island?"

The police officer laughed, glanced through the open door, and lowered her voice. "Not recently. To tell you the truth, that's sort of a touchy subject. You know he's made a very generous donation to the police department."

Josie nodded. "The forensic center, yes."

"Well, we don't give him tickets because of that." She shrugged. "I don't approve, but there's not much I can do about it except express my disapproval, and no one here listens to me. Although, come to think of it, I haven't caught him speeding in a month or so."

"But do you know if Chief Rodney ever stopped him for speeding?"

"He sure did. Back in the winter. Apparently that's when they met. I don't know what there was about that meeting that led to his donation to the department, but apparently Chief Rodney impressed the hell out of Seymour Higgins."

"You know, I think that's exactly what happened," Josie said and continued on her way.

Chief Rodney was napping at his desk. Josie stood in the open doorway to his office, watching his chest rise and fall as he snored, and thinking about what she was about to do. This man had absolutely no respect for her. She couldn't remember if he had ever believed something just because she said it was true. Now she was going to tell him one of the last things he wanted to hear and she had to convince him that what she was saying was the truth. But, first, she had to wake him up.

"Hemmm. Hemmm." She cleared her throat.

Too soft.

She knocked on the nice walnut woodwork that she herself had installed.

No response.

"Chief Rodney . . . I need to talk to you. Chief Rodney."

One eye opened. "Miss Pigeon."

"Yes. It's me. I need to talk to you," she repeated.

"Whatever you say damn well better be important." Both eyes were open now and they were glaring at her.

"Yes. You need to arrest Seymour Higgins. He's a murderer."

The roar that resulted from her statement brought Trish Petric running into the room. "Chief, can I do anything?"

"You can lock up this redheaded idiot for interfering with legitimate police business."

"I don't think I can do that, Chief. May I ask why are you here, Ms. Pigeon?"

"I was just beginning to explain to Chief Rodney that I believe Seymour Higgins killed the man we found in the Bride's Secret Bed and Breakfast. Or, if Mr. Higgins didn't kill the man himself, he caused him to be killed."

"Do you know who the dead man is, Miss Pigeon?"

"No, but . . ."

"Then you're talking complete nonsense," Chief Rodney exclaimed and got out of his chair.

"But his identity doesn't matter. I know what happened . . . where are you going?" Josie asked. "Aren't you at least going to listen to what I have to say?"

"Of course he is," Trish Petric answered. "Chief Rodney knows he cannot ignore a citizen who comes to him with information relating to a serious unsolved crime."

He sat back down and scowled at the women standing before him. "Yeah. That. This better be good, Miss Pigeon."

"Maybe so good that you'll remember to call me Ms. Pigeon," she answered and got down to business.

"Now a lot of what I have to tell you is just speculation, but if you listen to it all, I think you'll agree that it makes sense—perfect sense," she added. Now that she had his attention, she wasn't sure how to begin. "You see, Tyler has been running all over the island interviewing working women for his senior project . . ."

"What the hell does that have to do with Seymour Higgins? You're not going to tell me that he's a woman in disguise, are you, Miss Pigeon?"

"No, but you see, Tyler doesn't want me to know what he's been doing, so he manipulated me—made sure I wouldn't be around when he needed privacy."

"So what the . . ."

"Which is exactly what Seymour Higgins has been doing to me—to you—to all of us. And he's managed to do it without even being on the island most of the time. Of course, he had other people do things for him. Rich people can do that."

"Who did what?" Trish Petric asked.

Chief Rodney just glared.

"Well, first he sent his grandson to draw up plans to remodel the Bride's Secret Bed and Breakfast, and then he sent his decorator to worry about those plans, and then he sent his wife, and then finally came here himself . . ."

"To do what, Miss Pigeon?"

"To cause you—and everyone else—to look at Island Contracting's crew for the killer." She took a deep breath and continued. "You see, everyone was worried about storage. The Bride's Secret is a huge place, and there was never going to be a shortage of storage despite the fact that it doesn't have a basement. But, by sending Luigi the decorator to make sure we understood that storage was of utmost importance, Seymour Higgins made sure we would be looking for extra space behind the walls."

"Which is when you found the body," Trish said.

"And those stupid dummies," Chief Rodney added.

"Exactly. They were stupid, but they served an important purpose. Their discovery meant that the police were at the site and interested in what Island Contracting was doing before the dead man was discovered." Josie turned to Trish Petric. "Seymour Higgins wanted to be sure the police connected the body with my job and my crew before the identification was made. He thought the island police would find their suspects on the island.

"That's also why he didn't just dump the body in the ocean or the bay. If the tide brought it back to land, everyone on the island would be a potential suspect. As it was, no one was looking outside of my crew."

Chief Rodney was scowling. "I don't get it, Miss Pigeon."

"Seymour Higgins is good at taking advantage of situations and when he came here in the spring he realized he had found something special—the Bride's Secret Bed and Breakfast, a contracting company insured by the company he owns, and . . ." She glanced over at Chief Rodney before continuing. ". . . And a police department that could be manipulated."

THIRTY-ONE

"**A**ND WHAT DID he say when you said that?" Sam asked, refilling Josie's wineglass and pushing a plate of Risa's homemade antipasto closer to her.

"I think if I'd been alone, he would have thrown me out of his office. But since Trish was there . . ." Josie paused and looked across the coffee table at Trish, who was enjoying Sam's wine as she listened to Josie's story for the second time that day. "He pretty much had to listen. There was a witness."

"So go on," Carol Birnbaum urged, entering the living room and putting a plate of freshly baked gougere on the table before sitting down. "Eat them while they're hot, but keep talking, my dear. We all want to know what has been going on."

"Okay. Well, to begin at the beginning, Seymour and Tilly Higgins visited the island last winter and they went to the Bride's Secret Bed and Breakfast. They met there when they were young, and she, at least, had a sentimental attachment to the place. She had also done a lot for her husband over the years—raised the children he had with his first wife, and more importantly, brought a lot of money into the family when they married. Her family was in the insurance business and as the result of their marriage, Seymour Higgins owns one of the largest insurance companies in the country.

"Anyway, when they discovered the place was for sale, she asked him to buy it, and he did—claiming it was a gift for her. She told Carol and me that she had always wanted a big beach home where the family could gather. But, in a very different way, the Bride's Secret Bed and Breakfast met her husband's needs as well . . . as did the situation here on the island.

"You see, Seymour Higgins was stopped by the police for speeding when they visited the island last winter. And my guess is that it didn't take long for him to realize what a self-important ass Chief Rodney is."

"Josie put this a bit more diplomatically when she was back at the station," Officer Petric interrupted.

"I should hope so," Sam said.

"Yes, well, Seymour Higgins's wife may have found the summer house of her dreams, but I think he thought he had found a place where he could do pretty much anything he wanted—and get away with it after spreading his money around a bit."

"The Rodney Island Forensic Center," Sam suggested.

"Exactly. So Seymour Higgins bought the Bride's Secret Bed and Breakfast to turn it into a vacation home for his family, but he had plans—private plans—to increase his worth at the same time."

"But. . ." Sam began.

"Look, I know this doesn't all make sense right now, but it will if you just listen to the entire story."

"It really will," Office Petric assured them, popping another gougere into her mouth.

"I certainly hope so," Carol said.

"When you say 'increase his worth,' you're talking about killing and hiding that man." Sam said.

"Yes. You see, Seymour Higgins's interests in the insurance industry meant he could insure his life and his partner's life as well—standard business practice—but, in this case, the death benefits were to go to Seymour himself. And he hired Island Contracting because he thought the police would suspect me—or a member of my crew—and not him.

"Look, you'll understand if you let me explain about the Bride's Secret. You see, Seymour Higgins didn't really care about the project at all. He hired my company without checking out our references, and then he allowed his grandson to draw the plans for the job. And Christopher, while a charming young man, is completely unqualified. I discovered that fact immediately. And then I realized Seymour Higgins had hired Island Contracting without thoroughly checking us out when he stopped by my office. All his research has been done at his office in the city, but that was enough for him to realize that our insurance situation gave him unusual power over Island Contracting. He was surprised by my collection of birdhouses because he had no idea that Island Contracting had done so much work. But our abilities didn't matter to him, because he didn't care how the house ended up. Seymour Higgins probably assumed the job wouldn't even get finished."

"What about his grandson's work?" Carol asked. "Didn't he care about the time and effort the boy had put into designing the remodeling job?"

"I don't know how Seymour Higgins felt about Christopher's work, but I know his grandmother was concerned about that very thing. She suspected something was wrong, which is why she spent so much time down at Island Contracting's office. She wasn't worried about storage—she told me that later—and she wasn't really looking for sinks and the like, although that's what she claimed at the time."

Carol nodded. "She was looking for information about your company. Yes, that makes sense."

"Exactly. She wanted Christopher's project to be a success, and she wanted the big family summer home that her husband had promised her—and she knew neither would happen if Island Contracting was an incompetent fly-by-night sort of company. So she was checking us out in a rather devious fashion, because she didn't want her husband—or me—to know what she was doing.

"But the real story starts when I hired Leslie, the second lucky break for Seymour Higgins."

"What about Leslie?" Carol asked.

Josie glanced at Sam. "There's something about Leslie that you don't know, but that Seymour Higgins did: he's uninsurable. He can't get health insurance."

"You have someone working on your crew who does not have health insurance? Do you know what sort of risk you're taking?" Sam asked.

"I knew you would be worried, so I didn't mention it to you," Josie said.

"Josie, I can't believe you wouldn't tell me about that."

"I didn't want to worry you," she repeated.

"Just like you, Sammy, did not tell Josie that you've decided you can't stay in this house once you're married—because you don't want her to worry," his mother pointed out.

"You what?"

"I think you need to get on with your explanation," Trish Petric suggested before Sam could reply. "I have to get back to the station fairly soon, and I assume you want me to tell you about my part in this story."

"Yes. I'll go on. The other thing you don't know is that Seymour Higgins's insurance company has insured Island Contracting for many years."

"So presumably he had access to this information about Leslie."

"Exactly. And knowing Leslie's medical situation, he probably suspected that Leslie needed money. But I don't think he would have realized that Leslie was willing to break the law to get it if he hadn't discovered that Leslie was loaning—for a price—his driver's license to minors wanting to buy beer."

"How did he know that?" Carol asked.

"He discovered Christopher using it," Josie answered. "He probably wasn't surprised. The family knew Christopher had been in trouble in college for his drinking. His grandmother mentioned it to me the day we met."

"I knew there was a drinking problem on the island after working here less than a week," said Officer Petric, "but I didn't know how much some young adults were contributing to the problem until I spent some time sitting in the parking lot at the Wawa, chatting with the kids there and checking IDs myself."

"There certainly is," Sam added. "I make sure everyone who works at my store checks and double-checks identification. In fact, I had a conversation about that very subject with Seymour Higgins in the spring. He was probably thinking about his grandson back then. I never thought it might be significant, to tell you the truth."

Josie just took a deep breath and continued. "Anyway, Leslie Coyne is an important person in my story. First—he's horrible. I don't think I've ever hired anyone so completely unscrupulous. He lives off of women he claims to love. When I realized that, I told myself it wasn't my problem, which is true, although it did make me awfully uncomfortable. But Sam discovered that Leslie was stealing from the Bride's Secret Bed and Breakfast and selling what he stole on the Internet—and that is my problem. Island Contracting cannot afford to be seen as hiring dishonest workers. Apparently that doesn't matter to Leslie. Leslie cares about very little besides himself and money. I doubt if it was difficult for Seymour Higgins to convince Leslie that it would be in his interests to help him out."

"And what exactly did Leslie do for Seymour Higgins?" Carol asked.

"In the first place, Leslie was present when all three bodies were found: the two dummies and the murdered man. I should have realized that immediately. In fact Officer Petric pointed it out to me, but I ignored her."

"You think Leslie knew where they were hidden?" Sam asked.

"Yes. He may even have hidden the dummies. I don't know about that, but Leslie certainly made sure they were found when they were."

"And Seymour Higgins paid him to do this," Sam continued.

"And to put his driver's license on the dead man!" Carol added enthusiastically. "But why would he do that?"

"I doubt if he did. I think that came as a complete surprise to Leslie. But Seymour Higgins wanted Leslie connected with the dead man. He expected Leslie to be arrested for the murder. But of course, he didn't realize we would be interested in Leslie for other reasons."

"Stealing and selling the contents of the Bride's Secret Bed and Breakfast on eBay," Sam said.

"Exactly. No one would have known about that if you hadn't been shopping for that furniture you love."

"To furnish your new, bigger house that you can now tell Josie about," Carol pointed out.

"Leslie Coyne is being questioned down at the station right now, so we'll know more about all of this in just a bit," Officer Petric added. "But I think you can assume that he won't be on this project any longer."

"He's an excellent electrician and carpenter," Josie said sadly. "And he may have broken Vicki's heart."

"Hearts do not break. Not really," Risa said. "And sometimes the hurt heart is a good lesson."

Josie thought about the wonderful summer job she was in the process of losing. She wasn't sure whether or not Risa's statement was true. Her own heart felt like it might be splitting at that very moment.

"What about Seymour's first wife? Did she have something to do with the bride who ran away? Or was the bride just a myth?" Carol asked when Josie was silent for a moment.

"I'm the person who has something to do with the runaway bride," Trish Petric spoke up. "And she was a real woman. In fact, she was my grandmother, and she's the reason I'm working here this summer. My family used to vacation on the island when I was growing up, and I heard the stories about the Bride's Secret Bed and Breakfast over and over. Of course, my family knew the bride's secret—that she had fallen in love with another man."

"So there's no ghost," Sam said.

"I knew ghost not real," Risa pointed out.

"No, but my grandmother was very real. She died only a year ago. She never returned here after her marriage to my grandfather, but she loved this island and raised me to love it as well. And although my grandfather never publicly took credit for the building he designed, I was always secretly proud of my connection to the Bride's Secret Bed and Breakfast. When the possibility of a summer job here came up, I couldn't resist applying for it. I have a lot of good memories of summers spent here."

Josie smiled. She had ended up here for the same reason.

"I'll be damned! You do look like the woman in the painting that used to hang in the hallway," Sam said.

Trish turned toward him. "I don't suppose you saw that painting among the things Leslie has been flogging on eBay," she said. "I've searched all over the Bride's Secret for it." She turned to Josie. "In fact, I was looking for it when you discovered me there the other night."

"You must have been surprised when I showed up," Josie said.

"I sure was. I even grabbed one of your dropcloths and tried to hide under it."

Josie chuckled. "Which is why you scared the hell out of me—you looked like the runaway bride holding it in your arms."

"And it's why I was so upset when you found the dead man dressed as the bride. We were exposed to murder victims during my training, but none of them were dressed up to resemble my grandmother."

"But why didn't you tell me who you were and just ask me about the painting?"

"When I heard about the money Seymour Higgins was donating to the police department, and I've known about it for weeks, I assumed it was a double bribe—to Chief Rodney, of course, but to you, too."

"I don't understand," Carol said.

"Josie always need money, but she would never take bribe," Risa insisted.

"Because Island Contracting was going to be hired to build the forensic center," Josie said, nodding. "That's why you thought it was a bribe to me."

"Yes. I didn't know exactly why Seymour Higgins would bribe you, but I couldn't trust you after I learned that Island Contracting was going to benefit from that man's supposed generosity."

"But why did he offer to build that stupid forensic center anyway?" Sam asked.

"I suppose he felt that it would pretty much guarantee the Rodney rats doing whatever he asked them to do. He made sure Leslie was brought down to the police station twice. Everyone assumed Leslie was going to be arrested for murder and no one was really looking for other suspects," Josie answered. Then, realizing what she had said, she slapped her hand across her mouth.

"The Rodney rats? That's what you call them?" Trish asked, sounding thrilled.

"I used to . . ." Josie admitted.

"How appropriate!"

THIRTY-TWO

"**W**HAT A FABULOUS wedding! There's never been anything like it on the island."

"Yes, but I've gained at least five pounds in the past twenty-four hours!"

"You know the rehearsal dinner was cooked by Josie's landlady."

"Really? I spent two years studying art in Tuscany and I've never had better Italian food."

"And this is the best lobster quiche I've ever had."

"And the crab . . . fabulous. Of course, with Basil Tilby catering, no one would expect anything but fabulous food and drink."

"Well, save some space in your stomach. Sam's mother is inviting everyone here to breakfast tomorrow morning. I hear most of the meal is coming directly from the best bakery on the island. Except for the homemade sour-cream coffee cake—apparently Carol has been baking and freezing dozens of cakes for the past few months."

"I haven't seen Carol yet, but I hope I do. I wanted to ask her about Josie's dress. I heard that she went all the way to New York City to buy it."

"Oh, I don't think that's possible. How could she afford to buy a dress in the city? After all, Island Contracting's client was arrested for murder only a few months ago."

"I know, but how lucky for her. I'll bet Josie never, ever thought she would end up remodeling her own home."

Josie slipped behind the two women who were happily discussing her wedding, her life, and her expectations while stuffing themselves full of Basil's best seafood and champagne. They seemed to be having a wonderful time.

Everyone seemed to be having a wonderful time at her wonderful wedding.

The guest list had included most of the island's full-time residents, many people who had worked on Island Contracting's crews in the past, old friends from Sam's years in New York City, and, of course, Josie's family. Too many had accepted for the service to be held in any church on the island, so Josie and Sam had crossed their fingers, prayed for good weather, and exchanged their vows on the beach. The sun had been shining since daybreak, and even if Josie did wear flip flops with her gown, at least they were appropriate for the venue.

Josie looked down at her dress and smiled. Who would have thought that she would be married in the very gown her new mother-in-law had worn when she married Sam's father? "That was before I joined Weight Watchers, my dear!" Carol had pointed out when she offered her the dress.

Josie looked around. And who would have thought that their wedding reception would be held in the newly remodeled Bride's Secret, or that the Bride's Secret was going to be her new home—a wedding present from Sam, who had paid her company to do the construction as well? The house looked beautiful, and if anyone noticed that the plaster on the top-floor walls was still damp, no one mentioned it.

Sam walked up and slipped an arm around Josie's waist and kissed her earlobe. "Happy?"

"Of course."

"You don't look it."

"I was thinking about Tilly Higgins," Josie answered. "She's probably still upset about her husband going to prison for murder."

"And destroying most of their wealth in all the years since they were married," Sam added.

"If Seymour Higgins had been able to collect the huge insurance payment for his partner's death as he planned on doing, they might be sitting here instead of us," she pointed out.

"Then we'd be together someplace else. This is a wonderful house, but it really doesn't matter where we are just as long as we're together, does it?"

Josie leaned her head on his shoulder. "No. You are absolutely, totally right about that."

"And what do you think about Tyler's wedding present to us?" Sam asked after taking a moment to kiss his bride.

Josie looked over at the long built-in buffet Island Contracting had constructed in the living room and the huge glass lamp that stood on it. "I think it's hideous, but it really is the thought that counts, isn't it?"

"Yes. It really, really is. And you know I plan to spend the rest of my life thinking about you and your son."

She looked up at him and smiled. Living with that lamp was a small price to pay for so much happiness, she decided.